4/10

SHAM
ROCK

SHAM ROCK

RALPH McINERNY

Minotaur Books ✹ New York

This is a work of fiction. All of the characters, organizations, and events portrayed in this novel are either products of the author's imagination or are used fictitiously.

SHAM ROCK. Copyright © 2010 by Ralph McInerny. All rights reserved. Printed in the United States of America. For information, address St. Martin's Press, 175 Fifth Avenue, New York, N.Y. 10010.

www.minotaurbooks.com

Library of Congress Cataloging-in-Publication Data

McInerny, Ralph M.
    Sham rock / Ralph McInerny.—1st ed.
        p. cm.—(Notre Dame series bk. 13)
    ISBN 978-0-312-58265-4
    1. Knight, Roger (Fictitious character)—Fiction.   2. Knight, Philip (Fictitious character)—Fiction.   3. College teachers—Fiction.   4. Private investigators—Fiction.
5. University of Notre Dame—Fiction.   6. South Bend (Ind.)—Fiction.   I. Title.
    PS3563.A31166S49 2010
    813'.54—dc22

                                                                    2009041528

First Edition: April 2010

10 9 8 7 6 5 4 3 2 1

For the redoubtable Hadley Arkes

PART ONE

BURYING THE
HATCHET

1   FROM AN AISLE SEAT ON THE LEFT side of the plane, David Williams had an imperfect vision of the campus as they descended toward the South Bend airport. The lady in the window seat pressed her face to the glass, all but obscuring his view. No matter. He sat back with a wry smile, remembering all the times he had come along this flight path in his own plane, always taking the controls for the landing once he had feasted his eyes on the Notre Dame campus. He felt like a Roman general who had fought one too many campaigns. There would be no triumphal welcome this time. Only a memento mori.

The plane touched down; there was the roar of reversed engines as they decelerated along the runway. He had a glimpse of the tower across from the terminal and of a few private craft anchored to the runway. That was where he had always directed his own plane after landing, off among the elite, not like the rest of men. Another bead on the rosary of his personal sorrowful mysteries.

When the plane reached the terminal and drew to a stop, there was a long delay while the unchecked bags were removed and arrayed so that passengers could grab them as they headed inside. Meanwhile they stood with bowed heads in the aisle for ten minutes, impatiently looking ahead to see when movement would begin. All the aggravation of commercial flights would be familiar to him from now on, at least until . . . Hope flared, then died.

Inside the terminal, past seats filled with people waiting to fly out, he went with the others through the revolving doors and up the graded walkway to the baggage carousel. Expectant faces awaited the arrivals, and soon, all around him, there were reunions, passengers being greeted, the babble of happiness. Fifteen minutes went by before a light flashed and the belt began to move. He did not join the jostling group gathered to watch for their baggage. Now that he was here, he was in no hurry, no hurry at all.

When he had his bag, having watched it go round twice until it was the only one unclaimed, he rolled it to the rental counter to get a car. The clerk was a woman no longer young on whom incompetence sat like a lifelong curse. Her name tag read GLORIA. She drew her lower lip between her teeth as she sought his name on her computer, her expression doubtful.

"Williams?"

"Williams." He half expected her to ask him to spell it.

When she found it, she glowed as if she had won the lottery. Meanwhile Dave, looking beyond her, could see the envelope with his name written on it with a felt-tip pen—but of course there were papers to sign.

He handed her a credit card, and she scanned it; her expression once more gave way to doubt. Gloria frowned and chewed on her lip. Her eyes when she looked at him were wide with confusion.

"It doesn't go through."

"Try this one." He slid another across the counter, and she traded for it with some reluctance.

The second card was accepted, thank God. He had started to feel a sudden kinship with the clerk.

While Gloria had trouble printing out the forms, he leaned against the counter and looked down the curved line of the terminal.

Nothing was familiar to him here. When was the last time he had flown into South Bend on a commercial flight? It was not a question he cared to dwell on since it called up the golden interval since that was no more.

He signed and initialed the forms which, in another lucky win, Gloria had produced."Thank you," he said when, at last, he had the envelope with his key in it.

"No problem." A relieved smile. There were no other customers to disturb the even tenor of her ways. A large paperback with a multicolored cover lay open next to her computer like a downed bird. He made out the author's name in electric blue. Casey Winthrop!

"How do you like it?"

Gloria pursed her lips and wagged her head. "It's a living."

"I meant the book."

"If I didn't read I'd go crazy."

"I know the feeling."

But any rapport he had established was gone. Gloria had taken the mention of her book as an accusation. Guilt is everywhere.

He found his car, got in, and sat for a moment smelling its newness. When he turned the ignition key he saw there were less than a thousand miles on the odometer. What was the average lifetime of a car as a rental? Ah well, cars, like everything else, are temporary.

The road he drove along after exiting the airport suggested a city in decay; large, once desirable houses had been converted into insurance agencies, doctors' offices, a palm reader. He passed a storefront with a huge sign announcing that checks were cashed there. It seemed to be a pawnshop as well.

The downtown area was a slight improvement. He crossed the

St. Joseph River and after several blocks turned north, headed for campus.

The avenue that led to campus was now lined with newly constructed houses, designed to look older than they were, the university's effort to reclaim the area by building homes for faculty at attractive prices.

He was caught by the stop sign at Angela Boulevard. Already he could see ahead the great mass of the Main Building and the golden dome on which Our Lady looked ever southward. The sight stirred him, as it always did, as it stirred all alumni, as if they had spent four years staring up at the patroness of Notre Dame.

The guard at the gate gave him a wary welcoming smile when he failed to see a sticker on the window.

"Visitor?"

"I have an appointment with the vice president." He adopted a reassuring smile. "Class of '89."

Did the guard think he meant the vice president? The delay was pro forma; Williams was given a pass.

"Put that in your window."

The bar lifted, and Williams, saluting, moved forward, onto the campus, past Cedar Grove Cemetery on his left with ahead the nine holes of Burke Golf Course that had not yet been claimed for new buildings. Despite the anguish of the past months, despite the reason for his coming, David Williams had the odd sense that he had come home.

2 IN HIS OFFICE IN BROWNSON, ONE of the oldest campus buildings, just behind Sacred Heart Basilica, Roger Knight was seated at his desk in a large chair, reading the note that he had found slipped under his door. He had moved it across the room with his foot so he could sit before attempting to pick it up. *Your days are numbered.*

Of course they are, and in many ways. By the calendar, by counting from his date of birth or any other date arbitrarily chosen. The message had been composed on a computer and printed out in a 24-point font. No addressee.

A joke? In a recent class he had spoken of the Julian and Gregorian calendars, prompted to do so by the dates in Russian novels, New Style, Old Style, anno Domini in either case. How much give was there in computing the number of years that had passed since the birth of Christ? On then to the distinction between numbering number and numbered number. Many of the students looked numb.

The bane of a capacious memory is that it delivers up items at random, some important, most not. A mixed blessing for a professor. Afterward Jay Williams had said, "That was interesting." There was the slightest trace of irony in the young man's voice.

Roger checked himself from giving the etymology of "interest." "It doesn't add much to one's appreciation of Gogol."

"The search engine?"

Roger winced.

"I wonder how old I would be by the Julian calendar, Professor?"

"The age you are."

"But—"

"It's why I distinguished between numbers and the things they number. Not that it's my distinction."

They had gone out of the building to Roger's golf cart, the vehicle in which he made his way around campus.

"How long does a charge last?" Jay asked.

"It depends on how much I use it."

The smile came slowly, but at least it came. Jay Williams was the kind of student who cultivated professors, always ready with a question and sometimes, as now, staying around after class was over. Still, some glib students were intelligent.

Now, in the hallway outside, there was the sound of approaching footsteps, quick, young. They stopped, and Roger could hear the key put into the lock of the office opposite his own. The door slammed, a minute or two went by, and then the door opened and there were footsteps and a pounding on Roger's door.

"Come in," Roger roared.

Still wearing her ankle-length coat, an alpine hat rakish on her head, Sarah Wiggins looked terrified. She was waving a sheet of paper.

"Don't tell me your days are numbered, too?"

She pushed a chair nearer the desk and sat, her eyes never leaving Roger's. "This is a joke?"

"It's hard to appraise a punch line apart from the context."

She thought about that. She unbuttoned her coat and began to pull out a seemingly endless scarf. "They're meeting tomorrow!"

"They" were the appointments and tenure committee of the department Sarah hoped to join permanently. Her husband was in the sciences; there had been no opening in English when they came to Notre Dame, no tenure track position, so Sarah had agreed to teach a few classes as an adjunct, with the understanding that she would have an inside track when a position opened. A position had opened, but to her dismay a notice had been placed in the *Chronicle of Higher Education,* drawing a flood of applications; two candidates had been invited to campus and made quite a stir. She had been asked to make a formal application, but the need to give a talk had been waived. Not that she took comfort from that.

"They know me too well, Roger. I'm damaged goods." She rattled the paper. "This is meant to prepare me."

Roger picked up his own copy of the enigmatic phrase and showed it to Sarah.

"Where did you get this?"

"Someone must have slipped it under my door."

A pretty face is seldom made prettier by a gaping mouth, but then the sparkle of relief in Sarah's eyes made up for it. She jumped to her feet, held the two sheets of paper side by side, and turned to the window.

"Are you looking for fingerprints?"

"There's a watermark."

"Would you like some coffee?"

"Is it made?"

"I thought that you might—"

She made a face. "You need a wife."

"You sound like God in Genesis."

Roger's coffeemaker could produce two cups at a time, if two pods were used. It was a much easier system than the Mr. Coffee it had replaced. It was the task of getting in and out of his chair that prompted Roger's suggestion. Sarah made coffee for them.

"Why would you think that message concerns your promotion?"

"Oh, you know why."

"Friend or foe?"

"Braxton." She made the name sound like a Bronx cheer.

Braxton was another medievalist, tenured, with whom Sarah had crossed swords.

"Isn't her speciality Provençal?"

"Roger, you don't understand medievalists."

"That's true."

"There's something else." She said this softly, looking toward the window. "I'm pregnant."

"Congratulations!"

"Can you tell?"

Roger was flustered. He had noticed no alteration in Sarah's appearance. "Surely you don't think that is an impediment."

"In Braxton's eyes I would be that woman in *Brave New World*, lost among the savages."

"Oh, come."

"Roger, you don't understand a certain kind of feminist."

"I don't understand any kind."

"Nonsense. You understand me."

"Are you a feminist?"

"Is the pope German? Of course I'm a feminist."

"I hadn't noticed."

Sarah had left the door open. At sounds in the hallway, she fell silent. They listened to shuffling feet, heard a door unlocked, waited. Some minutes later, shuffling steps approached, and then old Emil Chadwick appeared in the doorway. He was holding a sheet of paper.

"Your days are numbered," Roger suggested.

Sarah took the sheet from Chadwick's hands and added it to the two she held. Chadwick seemed unsurprised, but then he was emeritus and was beyond surprise. Sarah studied the three sheets.

"What does it mean?" she asked, ceding the chair to Chadwick.

"Construction will soon begin."

Sarah's mouth was once more agape; she turned to Roger and began to nod. "Of course."

The suggestion seemed the basis of a consensus. A new building was scheduled to rise on land that had once been the laundry but for years had served as a parking lot providing convenient spaces for the motley crew who had offices in Brownson. At the beginning of the fall semester the announcement had been made, arriving to those affected like a judgment from Oz. A new ethics center would be built between Brownson and the Grotto. However surprising, the judgment was final, written in stone before a stone was laid.

Chadwick had counseled against raising a protest. "It will only increase their pleasure. Arbitrary power craves opposition."

"Where will you park?" Sarah asked Chadwick, real concern in her voice.

He tipped his head to one side and then the other. "My days are numbered." He took a package of cigarettes from his pocket, and Sarah, horrified, fled.

"Do you mind?" Chadwick asked Roger.

Half an hour later Roger was alone. The three sheets of paper lay on his desk where Chadwick had thrown them as if they were a poker hand. Three of a kind. One message and three interpretations.

3 A FINANCIAL ADVISER LEARNS TO radiate confidence whether he feels it or not, but David Williams, talking with Fenway in the Notre Dame Foundation, doubted that his manner was convincing.

"Of course, many have been hit pretty hard," Fenway said.

"Has the university been affected?"

"Surprisingly little, but then we've always had a conservative investment policy."

Williams nodded. What a smug bastard Fenway was. Williams had always described his own operation as conservative, prudent. Indeed, it had been. The tsunami that had swept away a significant fraction of his personal wealth as well as much that had been entrusted to him by others had come as an act of God. Overnight, it sometimes seemed, blue chips plummeted, the most solid investments melted away, great firms folded, banks closed, there was panic in Congress and in the administration. Of course, reversal had always been a logical possibility. What goes up can come down. Reminding clients of such elementary truths, he had ceased believing in them himself, as if the law of gravity had been abrogated. So many simple truths had been brought home by the crash.

"How much of a delay are you thinking of?" Fenway asked.

"Construction hasn't started, has it?"

"Oh my, no. We never begin building until we have three-quarters of the total cost in hand."

"A wise policy. I would say half a year at least."

A guess, of course. How demeaning to have to say this to Fenway. In their earlier meetings, Williams had been a golden boy of the financial world, one of the alumni the foundation had courted.

Fenway nodded. "Then we won't look for alternative donors."

Alternative donors for the proposed Williams Center for Ethics? Of course, it would be named for him only if he came up with the amount he had pledged. There was some consolation to be derived from the fact that his schedule of donations had not kicked in before the roof fell in on him.

It was sobering to think that it was less than a year ago that he had sat in this very office and worked out the details with Fenway. Afterward, he had been taken to the provost and then the president and thanked for his generosity. Had he imagined that all that praise and gratitude amounted to a plenary indulgence? He was sure that Fenway would not want to parade him through the Main Building today. He felt like a welsher, even though he wasn't. For months now he had been reviewing his moves, the advice he had given, and even in retrospect it all seemed sensible. Would he advise differently today—if people continued to entrust their money to him?

It was difficult to know how much Fenway guessed about his circumstances. Some of his clients were in revolt, and he could hardly blame them. Those he had acquired through Mame Childers were taking the downturn stoically enough. Only Briggs, a Domer who had graduated a few years after Dave, was suddenly aghast at what was happening to his investments . He had become almost unstrung when the decline had taken 20 percent of what he had entrusted to Dave. At the outset, Briggs had specified that he didn't want to invest in any morally questionable corporations.

"No bioengineering!" Briggs was taller than he seemed, but then he had the look of an alighting bird when he appeared at Dave's office. Dave agreed, no bioengineering.

The money they were talking about had come to Briggs from his wife, Philippa, a pudgy little lady with a pursy smile. Briggs and his wife had sold off her father's wholesale liquor business for a very large number and turned it over to Dave.

"I don't want to think about it, Dave."

"I'll do the thinking."

The problem was that Briggs didn't have a lot to think about apart from his investments. Several times a week he came to the office, just curious, how we doing, how are things going? Della Portiere, Dave's administrative assistant, would put Briggs in a little room where he could watch the fluctuating prices of stocks fly by on the screen. He even grew philosophical about what those altering numbers meant.

"Zillions of sales all over the country all day long. How can they talk of the 'market' as if it were someone?"

It was true, they all did talk that way. When trading was over for the day there was speculation as to what the market was saying, what it was reacting to, pondering the matter as ancient Romans had probed the entrails of birds.

"It *is* someone, Larry. It's you, me, and all the others."

An interested client is an interesting thing, up to a point. Briggs became a pain in the neck. He would have liked weekly reports, daily reports, if Dave had been willing to supply them. Still, all had gone well while Briggs's investments were increasing in value. Besides, Briggs could always be diverted by talk about Notre Dame.

"Your son's out there, isn't he?" he asked Dave.

"Junior year."

"So you trust the place?"

"What do you mean?"

Briggs's eyes narrowed. "It's no longer the school I attended."

"The football team will come back."

Possibly, but it was the secular drift of the university that pained Briggs. He had stories. He had informants. He was outraged about all the waffling on the *Vagina Monologues*.

"I didn't know they could talk, Larry."

All wrong. Larry was serious, very serious. The current administration at Notre Dame was betraying his alma mater. With any other alumnus, Dave might have discussed such matters, but Larry Briggs was too intense. The decline in the value of his investments had robbed him of any sense of humor he might have had.

"Almost every day," Della said when he asked her about Briggs. "He wants to know how your other clients are doing."

No need to tell Della not to feed Briggs's curiosity. "Set up an appointment, Della."

Sometimes he felt that he had become Briggs's therapist. Briggs acted like a bettor at the track who wanted his money back after his horse had lost. Well, Dave felt the same way. Maybe he could get some of the money the government was throwing around. Successful as he had been, his operation was minuscule compared to the giants who had fallen. He had actually thought of making a first payment on this visit to Notre Dame, as a matter of honor, or perhaps of self-deception, but Fenway's condescension drove that thought away.

"A half year at the outside," he said.

"Of course. Keep me posted."

"I suppose you've had lots of this."

Fenway's brows rose in a question.

"Postponed gifts."

"You'd be surprised," Fenway said. He didn't say how.

Outside Grace, a chill wind caught him, and Williams drew his coat close about him. He wished now he had called Fenway, convinced that on the phone he could have handled the situation better. Even so, he felt relief that he was relieved, if only for the present, of his pledge to the university. When he had made it, there had been an item on the Notre Dame Web page. David Williams, Class of 1989, pledges twenty million dollars for new ethics center building. At least Fenway hadn't reminded him of that.

He turned, shielding himself from the wind, and got out his cell phone. Call Jay? Thoughts of Mame assailed him. Moreover, his son had of late adopted a condescending attitude toward the way he made a living.

"Usury, Dad."

"Nonsense."

"Money shouldn't make more money."

"Thank God it does." Or at least it had.

He scrolled through his addresses. Ah. Father Carmody. He punched the number.

4 AS A MEMBER OF THE CONGREGATION
of Holy Cross, Father Carmody had taken the
three vows of religion. That had been long, long ago, and none of
those vows had sat heavily on his shoulders over the years. Poverty,
chastity, obedience. Well, maybe obedience, but then he had always
been in the inner circle, commanding obedience rather than observing it. Through a series of presidencies he had been a man in
the background, the éminence grise, finding unperceived power
more satisfying than the public kind. However, that role had dimin-
ished of late; indeed, under the new administration it had all but
disappeared. The calls on his presumed wisdom had declined ever
since he voiced concern about concentration on the university's endowment. The sum had risen astronomically, and its further increase
seemed to become an end in itself.

"What would you suggest, Father?"

"Using it. Lower the tuition, for example."

This obvious suggestion had been regarded as Pickwickian. Or
would have been if anyone still read Dickens. Try naive.

What could the vow of poverty mean if it were lived in an in-
creasingly rich institution? Not that poverty had ever had much bite
to it. It had come to mean lack of concern for the source of the
money that provided them a carefree existence. Everyone had his

own automobile now, traveled at will, lacked nothing really. Three squares and a good bed didn't begin to cover it.

"Not everyone has taken the vow of poverty, Father."

The laypeople in the administration certainly hadn't. They were remunerated on the scale of officers in a major corporation, heady sums, plus all the perks of office. Faculty salaries, too, had risen to giddy heights, even as fewer demands were made on professors. Perhaps the adjunct faculty could be called poor, those temporaries who enabled the tenured faculty to reduce what was referred to as their teaching "load." The term suggested that the faculty were hod carriers, sweating under their burden. That burden was typically two courses a semester now, scheduled on two days of the week. When retirement came, who would be able to tell the difference?

"It frees them for research, Father."

"Research" had become a sacred term. "A national Catholic research university" was now the preferred description of the place. Why not simply "scholarship"? "Research" suggested to Carmody someone in a lab coat frowning at a beaker held up to the light. Around 1920, Father Nieuwland had discovered the formula for synthetic rubber, and a mural depicting the man at work in his laboratory had adorned a wall in the pay cafeteria in the South Dining Hall. What could be the equivalent of that in theology or English or history? Oh, he knew the responses to that, having groused about it often enough.

Had he become a crank? He had certainly become old. He lived now in Holy Cross House across the lake from campus, where elderly members of the Congregation went to spend their final years. How many of the faculty did he know now? Or members of the administration, for that matter. It was difficult to avoid the realization that he had been put out to pasture. Not that he considered himself a typical resident of Holy Cross House. His health was good, thanks to a lifetime of smoking and intermittent total abstinence. He still had a lot of miles in him, but what was the good of that if he wasn't called upon? Thank God for Roger and Phil Knight.

One of his last contributions to the university was to get the endowed chair that had brought Roger to Notre Dame. The chair was named after Huneker, a Philadelphia author, mainly music criticism, whose work not even the descendants who had come up with the money for the chair had read, or were ever likely to. It was the thought of their name being commemorated by an endowed chair that swayed them. No need to dwell on Huneker's less than edifying life. Not much of a Catholic when the chips were down. Never mind; the object was to have a place into which the corpulent Roger could be put.

There had been opposition, of course. The faculty no longer sat still for appointments made from on high. That had been turned to Roger's advantage. He was what he himself called a free variable, a member of no department, an entity unto himself who taught whatever he felt fitted under the aegis of Catholic Studies.

Father Carmody's last coup, as it now seemed, was to direct the money Dave Williams wanted to give the university into support for the Center for Ethics and Culture. What might the center not do with a new building and secure funding? How odd that he was thinking of that when Dave Williams called.

"Long time no see."

"How about now, Father?"

"Now? Are you on campus?"

He was. Carmody told him to come ahead.

He went outside the front entrance and claimed the chair in which Ted Hesburgh smoked his evening cigar.

There had been talk in recent weeks about the country's financial situation. Only old Keenan could have pretended to understand what was going on, but he was deep in dementia, beyond the economics that had occupied him in the classroom. His last pronouncement had been that the country was going to hell in a handbasket. He meant financially. It was too bad he wasn't lucid enough to see his prediction coming true.

In a previous conversation, Dave Williams had dismissed such fears. "There are too many safeguards, Father. Regulations, watchdogs. The country learned its lesson from the Great Depression."

Carmody had no independent view on that. After all, he was told that the universe had been expanding ever since the Big Bang. It seemed to be a theological point that eventually there would be a great collapse.

Ten minutes after Father Carmody settled into his chair, Dave Williams drove up, parked, and came bouncing across to him.

They talked in Carmody's room; they went on to Sorin's in the Morris Inn; afterward they would stop by the Knights'.

"It's bad, Father." The bounce had gone out of Dave when they settled down to talk.

By the time they got to the Morris Inn, Carmody had the impression that Dave was ruined.

"Oh, no. Personally, I'm not in bad shape. I may soon be out of business, though."

And do what?

Dave didn't know. He seemed almost bewildered. "I may be sued." To his credit he seemed at least as dismayed by the fate of his clients. "Of course, I have to postpone my gift for the ethics building."

"We don't need an ethics building."

"But you argued for it."

"Only to prevent your money from going to something else. There are too damned many new buildings as it is."

5

JUST AS BOOK DEALERS ARE REGU-
larly approached by owners of old but worth-
less books, thinking they have a treasure, so the archivist's
professional appraisal of gifts will often differ from the donor's as-
sumptions. Greg Walsh, associate archivist at Notre Dame, had come
to regard donations from old grads with skepticism. Memorabilia of
old sports events were a constant item, but how many accounts
of the famous 10–10 tie between Notre Dame and Michigan State
do you need? Letters were another thing, and diaries even better.
Greg had been puzzled when the neatly wrapped package arrived
from Our Lady of Gethsemani, a Trappist abbey in Kentucky.
Cheese? No, it contained items that Patrick Pelligrino, now Brother
Joachim, Notre Dame '89, hoped the archives would find of interest.
Greg put them away for a duller day, when he could pore over the
contents, hopeful that the box contained good things.

It was on a rainy Saturday afternoon, in an empty archives, that
Greg again opened the box. Among the things it contained was a
sealed manila envelope, bulky, and a slimmer addressed envelope.
He set them aside and sorted through the playbills and course
notes, a dozen newspaper clippings about a missing student, and
a diary that disappointed since the entries were sparse, scattered

through the little book with a padded cover on which "1988" was embossed in faded gold. Finally he opened the larger sealed envelope. The sheaf of elegantly handwritten pages bore the printed title *De mortuis nil nisi bonum*. Speak well of the dead. It proved to be a story, and it was dedicated "To Timothy Quinn, *requiescat in pace*." The newspaper clippings had concerned the disappearance of Quinn. Arranged chronologically, they moved from first notices of the missing Notre Dame student through the attempts to discover where he was to the announcement some months later that the search had been ended. Timothy Quinn was presumed dead, although his remains had never been found. Greg settled back and, without great anticipation, began to read the story.

The setting was the Notre Dame campus, the time some decades ago, and the story told of the rivalry of several young men for the attentions of the same girl. The narrator was Patrick, who was enamored of Beth, and his rivals were Dave and Timothy. The plot seemed to turn on which of them would win the girl, and the narrator developed nicely the way a common love had led to a falling-out among the three friends, the turning point being when Patrick became the distraught girl's unwilling confidante. Her trouble was not stated explicitly, but it seemed clear that she had become pregnant. By whom? Not the narrator, who is crushed by what the girl tells him. Having consoled her as best he can, he hurries off to confront Timothy and tell him that he must do the honorable thing. A vivid word picture of Timothy's enraged reaction makes it clear that he is not the villain. If neither of them, then who? David. The shared knowledge makes allies of the two until Patrick realizes that Timothy has violence in mind. He takes from the wall on which it hangs a hatchet, an award he had won as a Boy Scout. Seeing that Timothy's rage has become homicidal, Patrick struggles with him, trying to wrest the hatchet from him. An enraged Timothy strikes Patrick, knocking him out. When the narrator comes to, he dashes to Dave's room. Dave is sitting on his bed, holding the hatchet.

"Where is he?"

"Gone."

The denouement was disappointing. Having brought his story to this pitch, Patrick all but abandoned it. "I never saw Timothy alive again after our struggle." The end? That seemed to be it. Not quite. A line was drawn across the page and then: "I buried him and his hatchet." Beneath were instructions on where the hatchet and body could be found buried near the Log Chapel.

The names of the characters in the story were the names of two of Pelligrino's classmates. Why would a monk write such a story? It seemed to be a fictionalized account of a real happening. The manuscript was one he must show Roger Knight. Meanwhile, he gathered all he could find in the archives about Quinn, most of it duplicates of what Brother Joachim had sent.

"Something interesting has come in," he said to Roger over the phone.

"Ah."

"Are you busy now?"

"You have piqued my interest."

To bring Roger across campus to the library on such a day as this was out of the question. If Mohammed could not come to the mountain, the mountain must go to him. In this case Roger was the mountain. Only for the Huneker Professor of Catholic Studies would Greg have removed something from the archives. Of course, the Joachim donation had not yet been officially registered. That was the small moral loophole through which Greg Walsh wriggled when he set off for the Knights' apartment with a carton on the passenger seat beside him.

Philip Knight was sprawled in a beanbag chair in front of the television, watching a game that seemed to give him pain. In far-off California, Southern Cal was inflicting yet another humiliation on the Fighting Irish. Roger took Greg into his study, and it was there that the Joachim donation was examined.

Greg presented the materials in order of increasing importance, first the newspaper clippings. The tale of Timothy Quinn prompted memories of more recent student disappearances, each of which had ended in the discovery of the body, both apparent suicides. The case of Timothy Quinn was different, very different.

After the newspaper clippings, Greg showed Roger the diary. The enormous Huneker Professor of Catholic Studies leafed through the little book, reading the scattered entries. Pelligrino had made constant use of initials. BH appeared to be a St. Mary's student, an object of interest to the three classmates, PP, TQ, and DW. She had appeared in several plays with the three young men. There was also a CW and an MS. Roger looked quizzically at Greg, who handed his friend the envelope.

"Have you read the story?" Roger asked as he took it.

"Yes."

It was difficult to tell if Roger, as he read, found it interesting. When the narrative collapsed without resolving its apparent point, he frowned.

Greg handed him the final typed page. It read, "The above is an account of the disappearance of Timothy Quinn. This weighs upon my soul." The writer went on to say that he had resolved to spend his life doing penance for the foul deed.

"Why?" Greg asked.

"I suppose many monks regard their lives as a form of penance for past sins."

"I meant penance for what."

It was inescapable that Brother Joachim counted on the contents of the box being read, most notably the abruptly ended story.

"No other manuscript?

"No."

"There is no mention of Quinn's death in the story."

"The hatchet and the body?"

"That seems to be what is weighing on his soul."

What was the point of all the obfuscation? A twenty-year-old disappearance, the writer apparently considering himself responsible, for that and even for the death of Timothy Quinn. Did the Trappist monk expect to be taken from the monastery, tried, and confined in another sort of cell? He was clearly pointing an accusing finger at David Williams.

Timothy Quinn's hatchet could be located by means of the large boulder that Patrick Pelligrino had carried to it. To mark the spot, to conceal it?

The following afternoon, Roger and Greg went in Roger's golf cart to the Log Chapel and then wandered west of it. They came upon the large rock described by Pelligrino. Was he directing them to a murder weapon?

The sealed letter in the box was addressed to David Williams.

What to do? Roger's suggestion was that they put that question to Father Carmody on the telephone.

The old priest listened to Roger's account, saying nothing, and even allowed the story to be read to him over the phone.

"I suppose you knew these boys, Father."

"In those days I knew everybody."

"Is that yes?"

Father Carmody grunted. "What do you intend to do?"

"Ask your advice."

The old priest took a moment. "Put it back in the archives. Bury it."

"Just that?"

"Patrick Pelligrino was the author of two plays that were put on."

"The plays in which he and DW and TQ appeared, along with BH?"

"Beth Hanrahan," the old priest said softly. "What you've read me sounds like an undergraduate effort that for some reason he wanted preserved in the archives."

"You think it is twenty years old?"

"The story reminds me of one of Pelligrino's plays, inspired by Poe. A man named Primo bricks his rival into a wall and then is haunted by what he thinks are moans from behind the bricks. This goes on for weeks. Finally he tears open the wall, goes into the chamber looking frantically for a body. All this is recounted in a note, read years later. The wall is once more opened, and there is the body of Primo. It was a powerful play. Melodramatic, of course, and incredible, but good acting can do much for a weak story."

One of the playbills in the carton was for *Behind the Bricks*. The author, Pelligrino, had played the role of Primo. The rival was David Williams.

Roger told the priest that there was another letter, addressed to David Williams, the name typed.

"You didn't open that one?"

"It was addressed to David Williams. I wonder where he is now?"

"David Williams? I see him from time to time. I could pass it on to him."

"Will you tell him about the story?"

"That depends."

It was a few days later that Father Carmody called to say he was stopping by with an old student, David Williams.

6

JAY WILLIAMS AND AMANDA ZIKOWSKI were in the Computer Cluster in DeBartolo, sharing a computer, or pretending to. It was here that Jay had come up with the idea of a note to be slipped under the door of Roger Knight's office.

"Jay, that's stupid."

"Of course it's stupid. I'm a philosophy major."

"I wish you'd never signed up for his class."

"Amanda, it was your idea."

"A stupid idea."

"You've become a philosopher."

It was Amanda's wide face with its luminous eyes and the blond hair arranged in some complicated way on her head that had first drawn Jay to her. Now minutes could go by before he noticed her exterior. It was the inner Amanda who fascinated him. And all her breathless talk about Roger Knight had made him jealous, nor had his first sight of the blimplike Huneker Professor of Catholic Studies driven away his jealousy. He knew how susceptible women are to the helpless male, and Roger Knight looked as if he needed twenty-four-hour assistance.

The class was interesting in a way, Aquinas's assimilation of Aristotle, but it was largely an hour and a half of tangents. Jay would have thought that the overweight professor was showing off, but that didn't seem to be it. In fact, he rejected the idea that his numerous excursions off the subject of the course were tangents. He attributed Jay's question about them to the fact that he was a philosophy major.

"What philosophy courses have you taken?"

"Before I became a major? A survey and then epistemology."

"Ah. And since?"

"I'm taking Philosophy of Science this semester."

"Isn't philosophy a science?"

"You're kidding."

"Do you think philosophy is a specialty?"

"Well, it's a major."

"You've put your finger on the problem with higher education."

Luckily Amanda had not been in on this conversation. Roger Knight had asked Jay to define science, and he had answered, "Physics, chemistry, biology, astronomy."

"But what makes them sciences? You will say the application of mathematics to the natural world. A good answer. Of course, you probably think this is a fifteenth-century innovation."

"You don't?"

"Only up to a point. Well, at last you will be reading Aristotle's *Physics*. Does the name Arthur Eddington mean anything to you?"

This was hard. Jay's grade point average was as close to a 4.0 as a B in biology permitted. With Roger Knight he felt like an illiterate idiot. He didn't like it.

"You remind me of myself at your age, Jay."

"My weight?"

Roger Knight had roared. "Actually I was a wraith of a lad. The avoirdupois came later. Hop in." Jay got onto the seat of the professor's golf cart, and it started off silently. "Where to?"

Jay shrugged. "Where are you going?"

"Home. Care to come along?"

That was how Jay met Roger's brother, Philip, the more or less retired private investigator.

"I worked with him," Roger said proudly.

"You were a private detective?"

"I still have a license. We both do."

This was too good to be true. He could hardly wait to tarnish Amanda's image of her favorite professor with this information. The great professor, great in every sense so far as Amanda was concerned, a onetime private eye.

"What were some of your cases?"

"One of my favorites involved our aunt Lucerne."

Jay listened with fascination, as if he were gathering evidence. The case they had been put on by their aunt involved a riddle, and then there was the case of a dog named Fetch.

"You should write them up," Jay urged.

"Not everyone would be as interested as you."

"Oh, I know all about that," Amanda said when he hurried to tell her about Roger Knight's past.

"You do?"

"He likes to talk about it. Sometimes I think he misses being a detective."

That was when Jay conceived the idea of testing Roger Knight's prowess. It would begin with a note with a mysterious message pushed under his office door.

"Jay, that's stupid."

"It's just the teaser. We complicate things by pushing an identical note under the doors of offices near his."

"What is the object?"

He looked at her. Oh, those luminous eyes. He couldn't say that he hoped to make a fool of Roger Knight. He didn't like the frown that was forming on Amanda's brow. "Just to let him show his stuff."

"I'll tell him."

"Amanda, he's been a detective. This will be child's play for him."

"Well, it's child's play, all right."

She didn't like it. She would like it even less if Jay's campaign showed that Roger Knight was mortal, fallible, not the paragon of wisdom she thought he was. It occurred to him that then she would despise Jay Williams, not Roger Knight.

Amanda reluctantly came with him when he slipped the notes under the office doors. At the next class he asked Roger Knight to explain again the difference between numbering and numbered number. Roger was delighted and went on and on until even Amanda looked bored, but Jay intended to play fair, more or less. Afterward he expected Amanda to be mollified.

"I as much as told him who had written the notes."

"Jay, do you seriously think he is losing sleep over that silly message?"

"You may be right."

No need to involve Amanda in step two of the plan. What he needed was a riddle, like the riddle in the case Aunt Lucerne had her nephews investigate. Her estranged husband had left her a Green Bay Packers fan cheesehead and a piggy bank on one side of which was taped *Your name* and on the other *MacLivid*.

"What was the solution?"

Roger smiled. "There was a Swiss bank account, in Lucerne, and the number was given in Roman numerals. MLIVID."

"Pretty obvious?"

"Pretty unintelligible. It's not a Roman number."

"Of course not. That's the point."

"If you say so."

7 ROGER TOLD PHIL THAT FATHER CAR-
mody would be stopping by, accompanied by
a David Williams.

"An alumnus?"

"Class of 1989."

"It has to be the same one."

"Father Carmody described him as a benefactor of the university. He's given the money to put up the building that will rob me of my parking place."

Roger, of course, had told Phil about the contents of the box Brother Joachim had sent to the archives and Greg had left with Roger, seemingly glad to get it out of his hands. It hadn't elicited much interest from Phil, even after he read the story and the final typed page.

"Did you check to see if the marker is there, Roger?"

"I drove along the road below Old College. There is a large rock where Joachim said there would be."

"All you have to do is dig up the body," Phil said wryly.

"Is that your suggestion?"

"No. Forget about it, Roger. Father Carmody would say the same."

"He already has."

———

Father Carmody didn't knock or ring the bell but came right in, as befitted a close friend. The man with him bore a prosperous look and seemed unsure why he was being brought to see the Knights.

"I have heard of you," he said to Roger, trying not to show surprise at Roger's bulk. "My son is in your class."

"Jay? Of course." Roger stepped back and squinted. "I see the resemblance."

Phil joined them, then got beer for himself and Williams. Roger and Father Carmody had coffee.

"This is left over from breakfast, Father."

"I like aged coffee."

"Jay says he has never taken a class like yours, Professor."

"That has the makings of an insult. You should have brought him along."

"I haven't seen him yet. I went first to Father Carmody. I am here to explain that I will have to postpone my promised gift to the university. The financial mess has given me a little trouble."

"I don't understand what is happening," Roger said.

Williams smiled sadly. "Who does?"

Phil said, "I have everything in government bonds and municipals."

"Lucky man. If you'd been my client I would have argued against that."

"I don't want to have to think about money."

Father Carmody, having tasted his coffee, lit a cigarette.

Williams was surprised. "I thought this was a smoke-free campus."

"It is, it is. I just like to contribute something for it to be free of. We can smoke in Holy Cross House, you know. The only smoke-free zone I'm interested in is in the other world."

The sound of the game on in the next room caught Williams's attention, and he and Phil drifted in there. Roger took Father Carmody into his study.

"This isn't the ideal way to show you this stuff. The stuff that was sent to the archives by Brother Joachim." Roger took an envelope from the box and handed it to Father Carmody.

"What's this?"

"What I told you about on the phone."

Father Carmody read it, indifferently at first and then with growing concern. When he had finished, he folded it carefully and returned it to the envelope. He didn't look at Roger. "What are you going to do about that?"

"That is my question to you."

Father Carmody thought. Whatever moral drama was going on in his mind, Roger knew that any judgment would be made according to its possible effect on Notre Dame. Father Carmody might be critical of this or that in the current administration's doings, but all that was on the surface, something that would pass away, while Notre Dame endured forever.

"Seal it and put it back in the archives."

Roger nodded. It was the answer he had expected, and it wasn't just self-serving. What could possibly arise out of a Trappist monk's fictional claim of responsibility for a fellow student who disappeared twenty years ago?

"This is the other letter."

He handed it to the priest, who glanced at the envelope. "David Williams."

"They seem to have been classmates."

"They were close friends. They were roommates."

Father Carmody tapped his forehead with the envelope. "Do you think he would repeat that suggestion of murder in this?"

"There's only one way to find out."

"If he does, I will regret giving Dave this letter."

"I have a letter for you," Father Carmody said brightly when they joined Phil and David Williams.

"For me?" Williams took the letter and looked at his name written on it.

"Who's it from?"

"Pat Pelligrino."

"But he's a monk."

"You don't have to read it now."

"Of course I'll read it now." Moments went by, though, before he opened the envelope. Two official sheets, looking like a legal document. Williams was stunned when he looked up. "He's made me his heir."

It was indeed a legal document, dated some twelve years before. Pelligrino had inherited an uncle's estate and, before entering the monastery, had made out this will, bequeathing everything to David Williams, effective immediately.

"He must have been very sure he had a vocation," Father Carmody said.

"I can't accept this!" Williams said in a strained voice.

"How much would it amount to?"

"I don't care."

"Why don't you evaluate what the uncle had before you decide."

"I have decided."

"Dave, all you can do is give it away yourself now. You'd want to know what you're giving away, wouldn't you?"

"Notre Dame can have it."

"It may amount to little."

"How did you get the letter, Father?"

"He knew the address of the university, Dave."

Suggesting that Brother Joachim would have sent the letter directly to David Williams if he knew his address. Perhaps he would have. Father Carmody would have said that he had no control over what others thought his statements implied.

The bequest amounted to a lot. Arturo Pelligrino, Patrick's uncle, had eschewed brokers and bought in such a conservative way that his holdings were largely unaffected by the current economic situation.

Then there was the gold.

There were those who succumbed to the blandishments of dealers in precious metals, who touted the stability of those metals against currencies. Arturo had succumbed; he had bought half a million dollars' worth of gold, whose current value was many times that.

There seemed no need to tell Williams that his benefactor had all but accused him of the murder of their common friend, Timothy Quinn.

8 SARAH WIGGINS LIKED THE COMPANY in Brownson, but the truth was that her office there was an outward sign of her secondary status. A not unimportant aspect of her hope to be given a tenured position would be a move to an office in Decio, where most of the members of her department were, making her a full-fledged member at last. For all that, it was lovely to have the chance of visiting with Roger Knight and the old curmudgeon Chadwick. They seemed always to be in their offices, particularly Chadwick, who was emeritus and, in his phrase, hors de combat.

"My dear, it is good to have the losing battles all behind one," Chadwick said, putting a match to his pipe. The tobacco smelled so good at first, but that didn't last, maybe because newly lit tobacco had to compete with all the pipefuls of the past whose ghosts haunted Chadwick's office.

"When did you join the faculty?"

"In 1955." His eyes were on her when he said it. "Before your parents were born, I suppose."

Good Lord. Sarah wouldn't have been more surprised if Chadwick had said he had been a contemporary of Father Sorin, the founder of Notre Dame. To her, 1955 sounded as long ago as 1842, and he was almost right about her parents' birth.

"What was it like then?"

"The same and different. That's a definition of analogy." Chadwick had taught philosophy and called himself a repentant professor. "It took me a lifetime to learn that I know nothing."

Chadwick's office was a chaos of books and papers and memorabilia. He told her about the old days. Father Hesburgh had been president; Frank O'Malley and Leo Ward were colleagues. "We all knew one another then. The fraternity of penury."

The student body had been all male when Chadwick came, and the faculty as well. Discipline was enforced. Football games were won. O'Shaughnessy Hall had opened just before Chadwick joined the faculty. There were fewer than half as many buildings then as now. He had taught six days a week.

"Six!"

"There were two sequences, Monday, Wednesday, Friday and Tuesday, Thursday, Saturday. Saturday classes were a problem on football weekends. So classes began an hour earlier."

That old Notre Dame was spoken of condescendingly now, but Chadwick was a distinguished scholar, author of eight books, one of which Sarah had heard of before she and Charlie came to Notre Dame. *The Unknown God: An Essay in Natural Theology.* Chadwick had spent sabbatical years in Europe, in Paris, in Rome, a term at Oxford. He had been a widower forever, as he put it. There was a photograph of his wife on his desk, emerging from scattered papers. "My Last Duchess. My late wife. In every sense, she was always tardy."

"She's beautiful."

"Isn't she?"

Chadwick dismissed Sarah's continuing anxiety about the note that had been slipped under their doors. *Your days are numbered.* "A prank, my dear. And a not very imaginative one."

40

Nor did Roger Knight encourage her concern. "A reminder that one's days are numbered is scarcely a threat."

"It is when you print it out and slip it under people's doors."

"Sarah, you have to understand the student mind."

"Do you?"

"What there is of it."

"You don't know it was a student."

He thought about it. "That's true. Any word on the articles you sent out?"

She shook her head. "Referees take forever, and even if they're accepted it will be a year and more before they appear. But just an acceptance would add to my résumé."

Publish or perish. Publish *and* perish in many cases. All the standards were subject to the interpretation of members of the appointments and tenure committee. They could arbitrarily decide that certain journals were not really journals. They were like an election board after a close contest.

Her husband, Charlie, wasn't much help. "You can be part-time at St. Mary's. Or Holy Cross College."

"Oh, Charlie."

He felt bad enough about having a tenured position while Sarah did piecework. From the time they had met, he had treated her as the smarter of the two. "I'm a technician, Sarah. You use your mind."

The letter from *Speculum* arrived at home. Sarah did not open it until Charlie returned, then asked him to. He blithely opened the letter, glanced at it, smiled. "Congratulations."

"Really?" She had already snatched the letter from him. An acceptance, and from *Speculum*!

She could hardly wait to let the department chair know; the following morning she was in the departmental office before he was, half an hour before, trying to control her eagerness, trying to act blasé.

"Very nice, very nice," Tuttle said, reading the photocopy of the letter she had made for him. "I'll see that the committee gets this."

When she left the office, there was the inevitable reaction and her spirits dropped. Tuttle hadn't exactly jumped into the air and clicked his heels. Of course, she had no idea where he stood on her case, but he was allegedly under the influence of Braxton. Not even Braxton could deny that *Speculum* was as good as it gets in medieval studies.

Chadwick's reaction was more satisfactory. As a Thomist, he had subscribed to *Speculum*, and there was a shelf of ancient copies in his office. "You must give me an offprint when it appears."

Would he still be alive? Shame on her. *Your days are numbered.*

She waited until Roger Knight came back from his afternoon class. When told her news, he looked as if he were about to embrace her, then looked sheepish. So she gave him a hug, or as much of one as she could. He made the coffee then and asked for a summary of her article.

"I'll print you out a copy."

"Good. Good."

Roger Knight's one publication was his monograph on Baron Corvo, which had been the excuse for offering him the Huneker Professorship of Catholic Studies. Sarah had read it; it was a delight, but Roger was not a publishing scholar. Yet he seemed to know everything. Who had said that the academic life was now geared to mediocrity? Most scholars knew more and more about less and less. Next to Roger Knight they seemed narrow. Of course, anyone would look narrow next to Roger.

The acceptance from *Speculum* drove away all her silly anxieties about the note under the door. She and Roger left together, going out to the parking lot beside Brownson. She went with him to his golf cart, where they went on talking until Roger noticed how low his vehicle seemed to be. No wonder. Someone had let the air out of all its tires.

Sarah just looked at him. "Come, I'll drive you home."

When they got to her car, they discovered that all the tires were flat.

"What about Chadwick?" Sarah asked, all her panic returning.

"Sarah, he cycles here from Holy Cross Village." Chadwick's three-wheeled cycle gave him a magic mobility that more than compensated for the hoots and stares his passage elicited.

"Roger, it couldn't possibly be . . ."

"Coincidences do not require causes, Sarah."

But she could see he didn't believe that this was a coincidence.

The next day they learned that a tire pump had been propped against Chadwick's door.

9 ------→ ALONG WITH ALL THE OTHER MEM-
bers, both town and gown, the onetime self-
described Old Bastards table had been cast into outer darkness by
the administrative ukase that had declared the University Club ex-
pendable. The announcement had met with indignant protests. A
committee had been formed to compile a report that would tell the
administration what the club meant to the faculty and staff and
alumni. The eventual report was the size of the Chicago telephone
directory. It had no effect. The club was doomed and, on schedule,
razed to make way for a monstrous new building.

Those with a tragic view of life, those convinced that we are well
advanced into the end times, perhaps found this incredible decision
less surprising, if not less painful. Others were still stunned a year
later. Members of the erstwhile aforementioned table averted their
eyes when they came along Notre Dame Avenue and passed the neo-
Soviet monstrosity that was arising on the sanctified site of the club.
Most of them had avoided the campus entirely during the dark weeks
when the wrecking ball smashed into the beloved building, reducing
it to rubble. Now, a year later, they convened in late afternoon at
Leahy's Lounge in the Morris Inn where Murph the bartender had
welcomed them, one or two at first, then others, finally the whole
group together once more and once more engaged in the morose de-
lectation of comparing the present unfavorably with the past.

"To crime," Armitage Shanks said, raising his glass.

Half a dozen arthritic liver-spotted hands raised their drinks.

"What have they done now?"

"They?" The hearing-impaired Potts narrowed his eyes as he asked.

"The administration."

"The only natural criminal class on campus."

Bingham gave a brief, tendentious account of the recently announced new ethics center to be built between Brownson Hall and the Grotto.

"That's a parking lot."

"It was once the site of St. Michael's Laundry."

"Where will all the vice presidents, associate and assistant vice presidents, and the vast locust army of the provost's office park?" The words rolled mellifluously off the tongue of Armitage Shanks.

"They can be bussed in from far-flung parking lots."

"We're overextended. How many buildings are under construction now?"

Throughout the campus the great cranes of construction companies stood high in the sky, looking like prehistoric beasts.

"They'll go belly up," Horvath said.

"Have you gone by Disneyland lately?"

This was Shanks's way of referring to Eddy Street Commons, the vast construction project under way on the southern edge of the campus. There would be a mall with restaurants and retail stores, residences of various kinds, God knows what else, half a mile of newness to rub against the sensibilities of the Old Bastards.

"An ethics center?" Potts cried. Horvath had written this on a napkin for him.

"In medio stat virtus," Shanks murmured.

Bingham, who had taught law, seemed to relish the prospect of an economic crash, but then his late wife had once won the Powerball. National economic news was a serious matter to most of these old men, retired, living on fixed incomes pegged to the modest salaries they had earned in the days before Notre Dame described itself as a national Catholic research university.

"They're searching for Catholics."

At a table along the wall, Neil Delaney was nursing a glass of merlot, his eye on one of the television sets. Three hunch-shouldered regulars sat on bar stools, arguing with Murph about some sport or other. The Old Bastards had brought together several tables and commanded the center of the room.

"The university endowment has taken a hit."

"Brandeis is selling off its art collection."

"The party's over," Bingham declared.

Potts and Horvath were trying to remember the name of the alumnus who had pledged the money for the proposed ethics center.

"Williams," Shanks said. "David Williams. I had the boy in class."

"What year was he?"

"'Eighty-nine, I think."

"How much did he give?"

Bingham knew and said it out loud. Horvath tried to whistle.

"What does he do, rob banks?"

"He is a financial adviser."

The memory of Potts, in the surprising way of an old man's memory, triggered by mention that Williams had graduated in 1989, delivered up a name. "Timothy Quinn. The student who disappeared."

Other memories zeroed in at this reminder, and the Old Bastards leaned toward one another, trying to piece together that long-ago episode. Timothy Quinn had vanished from the campus, and no trace of him was ever found. The names of others involved were recalled.

"One became a Trappist."

"Chadwick's son?"

"No." Potts closed his eyes. "Pelican. Pericolo."

"Pelligrino!" cried Horvath.

"Patrick Pelligrino."

Shanks thought he had had him in class as well. "He wrote plays."

"For the football team?"

A fateful remark. The collective discontent was diverted to discussion of the football team, and the topic of the long-ago disappearance of Timothy Quinn was tabled.

10

DAVE WILLIAMS DROPPED FATHER Carmody off at Holy Cross House after a silent drive from the Knights' apartment. Before the old priest got out he said, "Lose some, win some, Dave. That money Pelligrino left you will mean a lot more to you now than it would have a year ago."

"You think I should drop by the foundation again?"

"I'll break your leg if you do. You told them half a year, take half a year."

"Father, I really don't think I can take this money."

"I do. In a way you have no choice. Don't forget, God has a sense of humor. You came here almost bust. You won't be leaving that way."

Old men take a lot of time to get out of a car, even old men who want to appear younger than they are. Father Carmody exited with grunts and groans, got the earth settled beneath his feet, and then marched toward the entrance of the building. How different his advice was now than it had been earlier.

"What's money except a bunch of IOUs from people you don't know?" he had said when they talked in his room at Holy Cross House. "Think of it as being robbed or having taken a bunch of bad debts. It's an opportunity, Dave. Where neither rust nor moth consumes nor thief breaks in to steal. I don't have to tell you what's really important and what isn't. Anyway, even broke, you're better off than ninety percent of the people."

Dave had needed that. Had he ever confessed greed or avarice? Yet his whole career seemed based on them, counting on those vices in others, acquiring them himself.

After leaving the priest at Holy Cross House, he drove to a parking lot near the Grotto and then sat on a bench looking at the replica of the shrine at Lourdes. There were hundreds of vigil lights aglow behind the image of Mary. Before her was a statue of Bernadette on her knees. He sat there comparing the gloom that had gathered around him during the past months with the view of life he had supposedly picked up as a student at Notre Dame. The financial crash seemed an external sign of his inner crumbling. He considered Father Carmody's words. God has a sense of humor. If there was a laugh here, it was on David Williams, that was for sure. How easy it was to conjure up Pelligrino's face, olive skin, thick black hair, almost good-looking, but something wrong with the symmetry of his face. Bags under his eyes even as a kid. Funny, Dave had considered suggesting that the new ethics center be named after Pelligrino.

When had the annual card from Brother Joachim started coming? A Christmas card of the more saccharine sort, the briefest of notes, and always the scriptural reference, carefully lettered in Latin. *Numquid narrabit aliquis in sepulchro misericordiam tuam et veritatem tuam in perditione.* Psalm 87:12. The first several times, Dave had assumed it was an expression of seasonal cheer.

"What's it mean, Dave?" Bridget had asked.

"I'll look it up."

He did look it up, but fortunately Bridget had forgotten it. "Shall thy goodness be declared in the tomb, thy truth in the land of the dead?" What this lugubrious thought was meant to convey, Dave hadn't a clue. Pat must be going stir-crazy in the monastery. At least

49

it wasn't the reference you saw on cards held up by zealots in stadiums, wanting to get the message onto TV.

What he had heard in the Knights' apartment made Pat's annual card seem an accusation.

During the months after Bridget's death, when his mind turned on the last things, Dave had considered getting out of the rat race, simplifying his life, doing something like what Beth Hanrahan had done. Maybe he would go to Minneapolis and help her ladle out soup to derelicts. Memories of Beth had made that seem unwise. Of course, it had been only a romantic dream. Good-bye to the world. He got over it.

After five minutes, he brought out the envelope and slowly read the bequest. It had been drawn up twelve years earlier, but Pat's uncle had left him the money twenty years ago. It had amounted to slightly over two million dollars then. What would it be today? Despite himself, Dave began to calculate what years of even uninspired investing would have done to that base sum. The Minneapolis law firm that drew up the document had entrusted it to a local bank, but even so . . . and then the gold! He could feel his reluctance drain away. He felt like one of the pirates in *Treasure Island*. Then the dread returned. The money was a more ominous message than the scriptural passage.

When he had pledged those millions to Notre Dame, Dave had thought that his generosity would offset the darker side of his life. Was Pat engaging in spiritual blackmail? How could he know how far Dave had drifted from the ideals of his youth, particularly since Bridget died?

———

From his room at the Morris Inn he called Jay and asked him to join him for supper.

"Dad! When did you get in?"

"This morning." A short silence. "I had a little business to take care of first."

"Hey, don't apologize."

Funny kid. "Was I apologizing?"

"There's a girl I'd like you to meet. Can I bring her along?"

"Of course."

With the girl, there would be no need to reassure Jay that everything was all right. All the gloom and doom in the news must have made his son wonder how things were with him. The fact that he hadn't called to ask could be read either way, of course.

He took a shower and a brief nap, forty winks as his father had called it. He decided to keep Pelligrino's bequest in his pocket. Where rust and moth consume . . .

The phone awoke him. Della. She would know that he had been on the job, buying, selling, looking for niches of safety for his clients in a volatile market. The computer he carried enabled him to conduct his business anywhere.

"What's up?"

A little silence. "Briggs."

"We're going to have to do something about him."

"I made a mistake, Dave."

"I doubt that."

"I told him you were in South Bend."

"So?"

"He's headed out there."

"Well, he's going to miss me. I leave in the morning."

Maybe it was the effect of that crazy story Pelligrino had sent to the archives. It was a lot easier to think of Briggs coming for him than it was to imagine Tim brandishing a hatchet.

When he went downstairs, he thought of going into the bar first—he had a quarter hour before Jay and the girl were due—but instead he took a chair in the lobby, off in a corner, where he could watch people coming in. There was a wall of books behind the chair. Props. Who would read a book while sitting in the lobby? Maybe they were there to take to your room.

The Morris Inn had been here when he was a student, not that he had often gone there. It had obviously been remodeled. Still, there was talk of replacing it with a grander hotel. Dave had stayed here with Bridget when they came for games; rooms in the Morris Inn were at a premium on game days, but he was already a significant benefactor of the university. The ache of loss had returned with a vengeance in recent months when things had gone into a spiral. There had been no one to whom he could express the fear he felt as the bottom seemed to drop out of a business that had always been on a rising line. Bridget had always been a worrywart about money. She never quite trusted the way he earned a living; it seemed so chancy to her. What was that saying? The vice of gambling and the virtue of insurance. Substitute investing. Couldn't he just salt it away somewhere, forget about making it grow? Maybe a coffee can buried in the backyard?

"Sweetheart, you spend the money and I'll earn it."

Ho ho. Bridget had never gotten the hang of spending money, though she had enough of her own. She hated it when he bought the plane.

"We don't own it, not personally, Bridget." That was technically true.

Because Bridget hadn't felt comfortable with affluence, she would have been a bulwark when things went bad. They never had gone bad before her cancer was diagnosed, though, and then eight months later she was dead. That should have brought the thoughts Father Carmody had suggested during their first conversation, but instead, after that brief romantic dream of chucking it all, he had thrown himself 24/7 into this business. Lately he had learned that somewhere along the line he had lost his self. His soul.

He crossed his arms and was aware of the envelope in his pocket. He could almost hear God laughing.

He didn't recognize Jay at first, but that was because of the girl. Dave rose from the chair and walked toward them. Jay took him in his arms, a big bear hug, but Dave's eyes were on the girl. Did Jay realize how much she looked like his mother? Jay had never stopped mourning her loss. What would he do if he knew about Mame Childers? What would Wilfrid Childers do?

11   THE HOUSE WAS NORTH OF TURTLE

Beach on Siesta Key, on stilts, with parking space under the first floor, which was a large rectangle with a kitchen and dining area at one end. Taking up roughly half the space was where Casey Winthrop worked, his computer on a trestle table, books all over the place, some in orange crates stacked along the wall, his own output ranged above those of the competition—one hundred and fifty titles, all of them paperback originals. One of the bedrooms upstairs had become a kind of sitting room where he and Peaches watched TV in the evenings, sipping wine, still camping out, at least in their own minds. Peaches was a wizard in the realty game, and Casey, well, Casey was a fiction machine and had been bringing in money like crazy for fifteen years. How much? He didn't really know. He didn't want to know, just as he didn't know for sure how many novels he had published. Who cares? It was the one he was working on currently that counted.

"I'm a hack," Casey would say proudly, and that is what it was, pride.

"Quit bragging," Peaches advised.

He was what he had set out to be. His idol even while he was still at Notre Dame had been John D. MacDonald. MacDonald had lived on Siesta Key, which was why he had settled here. At Notre Dame, Casey had been on the board of the Sophomore Literary Festival and tried in vain to get writers someone had heard of invited, writers who were read. The resistance to that sensible suggestion had been the seed of his vocation. Classmates were enrolled in writing courses turning out opaque stories that began nowhere and ended in the same place. Art? Literature? Being readable was apparently a crime. Caring about the reader was selling out. Casey began to send out things to the pulp magazines, of which there were still a few around then, and he collected Gold Medal Books, Ace Books, other paperback originals. He found an article about John D. MacDonald, all of whose titles he eventually collected. He sent the author a fan letter. It was never answered, but his stories began to be accepted. The die was cast. A year out of Notre Dame, he came to Siesta Key, for the winter. He never left. He rented at first and then, when he began to make real money, bought this place. The fact that Peaches loved it from the first time she saw it was a plus.

It was a throwback, the kind of place that had been built along the southern end of the key before the developments began. The owner who had slapped up the house would sell only when Casey convinced him he wasn't fronting for some developer.

"It's what I've always wanted," Casey assured him.

"The view of the gulf?"

"That, too." It reminded him of MacDonald's place, now the site of a gated community. He was regularly offered a fortune for the house—for the site, not the building; that would doubtless be knocked down and replaced by some high-rise monstrosity. MacDonald had seen the beginning of this and dealt with it in his novel *Condominium*. It was the first novel of his that came out in hardback, which Casey regarded as a kind of betrayal. Then MacDonald was written up in *Time*. His work suffered. Hack writers flourish in anonymity, if not neglect. Casey felt that he was picking up a fallen flag, like Prince Andrei.

He and Peaches lived the way he had when he was poor, keeping the trestle table and the orange crate book shelves and the cruddy comfortable furniture. At the beginning he had worked on an electric typewriter, but that, of course, had given way to a computer. What would MacDonald's generation have done if they had been able to write on computers?

"We're radical chic," Peaches said, one finger in an Edith Wharton, her glass of wine held before her as if she were checking for impurities. Well, it was a cheap wine. Never pay more than ten dollars for a bottle of wine. Casey seldom paid as much. He had bought some bummers, but basically wine was wine.

"I'm the chic of Araby."

He knew what she meant. He bragged about being a hack, and their lifestyle was based on little more than the pittance they'd got by on when they first married. Of course, they bought more books now that it wasn't really a luxury for them. What Peaches called the library was on the second floor, filling two of the three bedrooms. Hermione Lee's life of Wharton had sent Peaches back to the novels.

"It's better than I remembered," she said of *The Age of Innocence.*

"Innocence is always better."

He had met her on one of the upper floors of the Main Street Bookstore in Sarasota, since closed, another sign of the last times. In Biography. One thing about bookstores, you can make a pest of yourself with impunity. Or with a pretty girl. She was wearing a baggy sweater that went below her hips, what used to be called pedal pushers, open-toed sandals with her nails bright with polish. He went around her several times, humming, scanning the shelves. He went into the next aisle so he could peek through and see her squinting at the books. When he came into her aisle again, he cried out. How had he missed the legend on her sweatshirt? Notre Dame!

"You a Domer?" he asked.

"What's a Domer?"

"Your sweatshirt."

"This old thing."

"I went to Notre Dame."

She squinted at him. It was the first time he noticed the chevrons that formed on her forehead. "Did you play football?"

"Without a helmet. I still have these hot flashes."

Careful, careful.

"Someone gave it to me."

"Your husband?"

"Not likely."

"Stingy?"

"I don't have one."

That was round one. He dallied and went to pay for his books while she was still at the counter.

"What did you buy?"

She turned the pile of books on the counter so he could read their spines. The top one was a life of Edith Wharton. Other lives of writers.

"I'm a writer," he told her.

"Come on."

"Where? There's a nice little place up the street."

The sepulchral clerk followed this with interest. Her glasses slipped off her nose but bounced on her bony chest thanks to the chain that held their bows. The girl in the Notre Dame sweatshirt shrugged, looked at her watch. "Okay." The clerk was getting her glasses back on her nose when they left.

"What do you write?"

"Fiction."

"Would I have read anything of yours?"

"My biography hasn't appeared yet."

They went up the street and had beer at an outside table. It was her day off.

"What do you do when you aren't reading?"

She sold real estate.

"What's unreal estate?"

Apparently he couldn't be too corny for her. He told her he lived on Siesta Key.

"So you're not a snowbird?"

"Hey, I'm practically a native. You're too young to know the Anne Murray song."

To his delight she began to sing it.

"Perfect pitch."

"I was going to say the same thing to you."

Marriages are made in bookstores; at least theirs had been. They went out; they lolled on the beach; he showed her his place.

"I live in town, a dumpy little apartment."

"This will be an improvement."

"Ha ha."

It was fate, they both knew it.

A month later she asked, "How old are you?"

"Two." Chevrons in response. "Life begins at forty."

She was twenty-eight. She wanted to hear about Notre Dame. So he told her about Mame and Beth and the trinity.

"The trinity?"

"It's what we called Pat Pelligrino, Tim Quinn, and Dave Williams."

She was from Toledo.

"One winter I said, that's enough of this, so I headed down I-75 and there was Sarasota. I liked the name, don't ask me why."

"So we could meet."

They were married in St. Michael's on Siesta Key. Where do Floridians go for a honeymoon? Chicago. They drove down to South Bend, and he showed her around the campus, explaining his life to her.

"When you're here, all you think about is getting out, but it's like getting a tattoo. Indelible."

She had put in two years in a municipal college and hated every minute of it. There was a houseful of siblings; her parents thought her move to Florida made sense. At the wedding, they were dressed for the North. Nice people, but illustrating the mystery of genetics. How had they produced Peaches? She told him later that her father hated Notre Dame.

"I thought I noticed the mark of the beast on him."

"He's gentle as a lamb. Too gentle. My mom runs the house."

On campus it was clear that she had not inherited her father's genes. She loved Notre Dame.

"All our kids will go here."

"They'll wear helmets if they do."

Their passion was the nineteenth century and early twentieth, American and British. All those popular writers who had become classics. Casey knew Trollope's autobiography by heart. A craftsman, a writer, burning it out. Like Dr. Johnson when he went to London and hacked for years. Of course, in those days hack writers had known Latin and Greek and based poems on those of Juvenal. Even so, Casey felt that he was carrying on in a noble tradition.

Dave Williams had been curious to know what kind of money he made writing, probably unimpressed by the house. Dave had a regal place over on Longboat Key. Or did he? Peaches had learned it was on the market through multiple listing.

"Because of his wife, I suppose. That's been a while, though."

Peaches shrugged. "I'm glad we didn't invest with him."

Dave had never pressed him on that, no doubt thinking there wouldn't have been enough money to bother about. When Bridget was still alive, they had gotten together several times while the Williamses were wintering at their place on Longboat Key. Of course the main topic had been Notre Dame, and their old friends.

"A Trappist monk?" Peaches had cried, when she first heard about Pat Pelligrino.

They heard from Brother Joachim at Christmas, just a card, but it was nice of him to keep in touch. Nice, too, to think that they had an advocate in a Trappist monastery.

It turned out that Dave was selling his boat, too, and that looked bad. On the other hand, he had got a lot of publicity about his twenty-million-dollar donation to Notre Dame. Then Dave called to say he was coming down.

"I may be closing on the house."

"We'll get together."

"You couldn't put me up, could you?"

"If you don't mind roughing it. You've seen this place." There was a cot in the third bedroom, and it sure wouldn't be Longboat Key.

There he was, bragging again.

12 DAVE WILLIAMS FLEW INTO SARASOTA-
Bradenton Airport, came into the waiting area,
went past the aquarium surrounded by kids, and took the escalator
down to baggage claim. He got his bag, picked up a rental car, and
crossed University Parkway to a motel and checked in. Since it was
before noon, he had to wait for his room to be ready.

When Della told him that Larry Briggs was going out to Notre
Dame, Dave had been Mr. Cool on the phone, but he didn't like it.
Briggs had been hit hard, no doubt about that, but so had lots of
other people. Briggs needed someone to blame, and who better than
his financial adviser? It wasn't much of a defense to tell Briggs he
had lost a lot himself.

"I am in your hands," Briggs had liked to say.

"I always consult you first."

"What do I know about the market?"

A good attitude in a client, he would have said. "You don't have
to follow my advice, Larry."

"Ha. You're a magician. Philippa can't believe how well we're
doing."

Dave had taken that occasion to issue the standard warnings.
Briggs had waved off the suggestion that he go maybe fifty-fifty on

safe and sorry, even sixty-forty, but Briggs was hooked on higher returns. At the first shiver in the market, he had again told Larry it might not be wise to have everything in the blue chips.

"What else is there?"

"Municipal bonds."

"What's that, sewer systems, bridges?"

"It's a small but safe return."

"Where would I be now if I'd done that a year ago?"

Dave gave him a guess.

Larry snorted. "Let's go on the way we are."

So why was he blaming his adviser when he hadn't taken his advice?

Flying off to Florida, he almost felt that he was fleeing from Larry Briggs.

He called Casey and listened to the phone ring six times. He was about to hang up when Casey answered.

"Yo."

"Dave Williams, Casey. I just got in. When can we get together?"

"I'm still working on my daily stint. How about you and me and Peaches having dinner on St. Armand's Circle tonight?"

"Great. Any chance of you and me talking before then?"

"You got wheels?"

"I've got wheels."

"Think you can find this place?"

"If I can't, I'll sue Garmin. Two o'clock all right?"

Two o'clock was fine. It also gave him time to reconsider his idea of telling Casey what had happened at Notre Dame. Not the money, no need to go into that unless he had to, but Roger Knight had shown him Pat Pelligrino's odd story and his claim of responsibility for the disappearance of Timothy Quinn.

"He can't be serious."

The bequest was more ominous than the annual card. During their senior year, they had drifted apart, he and Pat, even though they continued to be roommates. There was an accusative look in Pat's eye. It was as if he were blaming Dave because Tim had decided to disappear.

"See much of Beth?"

"Do you?"

Answer a question with a question when you don't know what to say. Beth's changed attitude was more difficult to take than Pat's. It was clear that she had written finis to their going together. Did she blame him for Tim, too?

Blurting out that he couldn't take the money Pat left him had surprised Father Carmody, but what else could he say? Even before he read the confessional story, he had suspected that Pat was up to something. Over the years, his enigmatic messages on his Christmas card had been vaguely disturbing. Of course, they had to refer to long ago, when they had known one another, when they had been roommates at Notre Dame, when they had been close as brothers. They had dominated student drama in those days, with Pat's spooky plays and with himself and Tim and Beth hogging the best roles. Casey and Mame had only got the crumbs. After the meeting in the Knights' apartment, when Dave had decided to stay another day on campus, he went to Washington Hall, whose stage had been the scene of their triumphs, but the door was locked. Maybe just as well. His memory had kicked in already and didn't need any further prods.

He walked past the Main Building and went into Sacred Heart, thinking he might just sit there and try to figure out what Pat was up to, but an officious little fellow with silver hair accosted him and wanted to know if he would like to be shown around. A guide. It made the church seem a museum. Dave shook him off and went up the left aisle, turned toward the sacristy, and went outside again. He hadn't even breathed an Ave.

Breathed an Ave. He remembered Bridget singing "Danny Boy," substituting "Davy," a nice lugubrious song. The lover returns to the grave of his beloved, and she hears his footsteps above her. "For you will bend and whisper that you love me, and I will rest in peace until you come to me." How hauntingly her voice had risen on those last notes. So long ago. Everything seemed so long ago.

He went down to the Grotto again, sat for a while, but his mind was too full of too many things. Of course he knew where he was going.

Flags flapped from Old College on the side of the building that faced the lake as Dave walked along the road. Then there was the Log Chapel. He slowed his pace, trying to feel nonchalant. Would a boulder still be there after all these years?

It was.

He felt drawn toward it, but he stopped himself, filled with dread. What in hell was buried there? Was anything? He beat it back to the Morris Inn, checked out, and headed for the airport. Sufficient for the day are the evils thereof. He had enough problems in the present without brooding over events of twenty years ago.

Casey was in shorts and a T-shirt, barefoot, hair wild as if he had been running his fingers through it. The place hadn't changed a bit.

"What a dump," Dave said, but he said it with a smile.

"Yeah? What does your office look like?"

"Good point." His office. He didn't want to think of his office. He could work anywhere with his computer and cell phone. Mame Childers had sent an e-mail telling him that Briggs was trying to get her to take part in a class action against him, treating it as a joke.

The printer was rattling away, spilling out Casey's morning stint.

"What is it?"

"I agreed to do some Westerns."

"Westerns! What do you know about Westerns?"

"About as much as Max Brand when he started."

"Let me see it."

"Not on your life. I don't even let Peaches read work in progress."

"This place is a step up from a dorm room."

"Come on, I'll show you where you'll be sleeping."

He had forgotten asking if he could stay here. Following Casey upstairs, he felt it would be rude to tell him he had taken a motel room.

The second floor was livable, even comfortable, if you liked living in a library.

"How many books do you own, Casey?"

"I never counted them."

Casey showed him the cot in the third bedroom. "You can pretend you're Brother Joachim."

So there was his opening, if he wanted it. "He gave some stuff to the Notre Dame archives."

"They've asked for my papers."

"You're kidding."

Casey laughed. "That was my reaction. I didn't know anyone there was following my career."

"You can't walk through an airport without being reminded."

"No kidding." Casey grinned as if he were surprised that he had millions of readers.

Downstairs again, Casey opened the refrigerator. "I have beer."

"Are you having one?"

"It's my reward for finishing my daily pages."

They took their beer out onto a veranda with a nice view of the Gulf.

"Casey, you've got it good."

"You said it was a dump."

"Envy. Do you ever spend any money?"

"That's Peaches's department."

"How is she?"

"Wait and see. What did Pat give to the archives?"

"Remember Quinn?"

Casey had to think. "Our missing classmate. I wonder what happened to him."

"Pat seems to be suggesting that he's buried by the Log Chapel."

"The Log Chapel." Casey shook his head. He had the look of an alumnus about to start remembering the good old days.

"A boulder marks the spot."

Still Casey did not react. Instead he said, "Pat could have become a writer, Dave. He already was one. I wonder why he didn't keep at it. How many years before he went into the monastery?"

Dave let it go. Maybe Casey's was the right reaction to Pat Pelligrino's veiled suggestion that Dave had killed Timothy Quinn. Where he should have headed, during his frantic peregrinations, was Gethsemani Abbey to ask Pat what the hell he was trying to do with that story, with the bequest. The fact was, he dreaded such an encounter.

"So you're selling your place?" Casey asked.

"Want to buy it? I'll throw in a boat."

"I thought you were closing on the condo."

"It fell through. I was practically giving it away, and they wanted another reduction."

"This is no time to sell a house. Ask Peaches."

The big surprise was that Peaches was pregnant. She was maybe ten years younger than Casey, so that wasn't the surprise. It was the thought of his own son, Jay, a student at Notre Dame, that hit him, and here was Casey expecting his first child.

"As far as I know."

Peaches stuck out her tongue at him. "So the deal on the house fell through," she said.

"Why don't you two buy it? If I'm going to be robbed, I'd rather be robbed by friends."

"We're happy where we are."

"How's the realty business?"

"The market is glutted. It's a good time to buy, but buyers are scarce."

"You're telling me."

"How's this slump affecting you, Dave?" Casey asked.

They were at table in the Columbia Restaurant on St. Armand's Circle on Lido Key. The place was full; no sign of a slump here. Casey poured the last of the wine and ordered another bottle.

"Casey!"

"Peaches, think of it as a class reunion. It's our duty to get bombed."

"Then I'm driving."

"Of course you are. And I'll take care of the approach shots."
His eyebrows danced like Groucho's.

"Do you still golf, Casey?"

"Only twice a week."

"You must be looking forward to retirement."

"I'm looking forward to Junior."

They drank to that. They drank to lots of things. Dave went back
with them to Siesta Key and his cot in the third bedroom, sleeping
in his shorts, feeling like an undergraduate again. He would check
out of the motel in the morning.

13 ┄┄┄┄➤ ROGER KNIGHT WAS IN A MEDITATIVE
mood, his thoughts crowding one another for
position, all of them having to do with the materials Greg Walsh had
received at the archives, with Father Carmody's suggestion that
those materials be consigned to the dusty oblivion of the archives
and forgotten, and with David Williams's odd reaction to the news
that he was the recipient of a regal bequest from a former classmate,
now a Trappist monk, who moreover had committed to paper a supposedly fictional account of the disappearance of a classmate, his
rival for a St. Mary's girl. The spot where the hatchet was supposedly buried might contain something more gruesome. Roger had told
Jay that he had met his father.

"He's giving a building to Notre Dame. A new ethics center," Jay
said.

"We already have an ethics center."

"But they don't have a building."

To Roger the proposed building meant being deprived of a parking space for the golf cart in which he got around campus. Ah, the
convenience of being able to wheel almost to his office door, take a
few steps involving only one stair, and a minute later lower himself
into the welcome embrace of his huge specially constructed desk
chair.

Jay was difficult to understand. He had come to Roger's seminar as the guest of the lovely Amanda, and he had hardly settled in before he began to ask questions, doubtless meant to impress her. Jay had that strange confidence of the almost illiterate, a philosophy major—but that seemed redundant. His manner was that of an amused onlooker for whom Roger and what he had to say seemed to constitute evidence of some crime. It was tempting to make Jay the target of the discontent he felt at the loss of his parking space.

There is a kind of student whose curiosity bespeaks incredulity, as if any response to a question would add to the ridiculousness of what was being discussed. So it had been with Roger's account of the ancient theory of the elements and their origin in the pre-Socratics. Empedocles had summed it up in his theory of the four elements, fire, air, earth, and water, with love and strife to generate activity, but Roger had driven the theory back to Thales and water, Anaximenes and air. Heraclitus and fire. Roger had suggested continuity with the modern periodic table of elements.

"Our current view," he had remarked. "Perhaps destined to go the way of these ancient views."

"Tell us about air," Jay had urged, and Roger, feeling manipulated, obliged to feed Jay's skepticism. Doubtless he had overstated the resemblance between those ancient views and the table students of chemistry nowadays memorized.

"The theory is essentially the same. However many, there is an alphabet from which the things of our experience are composed."

Jay Williams smiled with tolerant incredulity, and Roger felt pusillanimous in noting Amanda's impatience with her admirer's attitude.

She had sought him out, apologetic. "I thought Jay would enjoy the course."

"And so he does."

"He's a philosophy major," she said, as if in exculpation.

It was the fact that the father, David Williams, was a financial adviser that had captured Roger's attention.

"You must explain the current chaos to me," Roger had said to him.

"I wish I could."

"I suppose this has affected your profession."

David Williams's eyes had lifted dramatically. But then, in his student days, he had been a regular feature on the stage of Washington Hall.

"Tell me about Brother Joachim," Roger had suggested. This was before he had insisted that David Williams read the confessional story written by Williams's old roommate, now Brother Joachim of Gethsemani Abbey in Kentucky.

"Brilliant," David had said. "The star of our class. You should read the plays he wrote, as a sophomore and junior. Incredible."

"*Behind the Bricks,*" Father Carmody had said. "A tour de force."

Greg Walsh had unearthed a copy of the play from the archives, and Roger read it with fascination. There was an odd triangulation at work here: David Williams and his classmates of yore, David Willliams in his present plight—Father Carmody had told Roger of the troubles in Williams's financial empire—and his son, Jay, with the commendable Amanda.

"Your name is a gerundive," he told her.

"Explain."

"She who must be loved."

No sooner had he said it than he felt embarrassed. Not that any woman student of his had ever misunderstood his chivalrous attitude toward the gentler sex. Roger thought in such phrases, with all the earnestness of the celibate. Phil had never married, and, as for Roger, he felt as eligible as Dr. Johnson for the role of swain. Call it sublimation, call it what you will, his regard for the female of the species, young, middle-aged, or mature, amounted to an idealization. Woman as the muse of man, half angel, a suggestion of a better world. The earthiest of poets had felt this, and Roger, no poet, felt it, too.

"Jay is your task," he said to Amanda. "You must be his Beatrice."

"I've been thinking about the disappearance of Timothy Quinn," Roger said to Father Carmody.

He had picked the old priest up at Holy Cross House, and they had gone to Leahy's in the Morris Inn, where Murph the bartender had some sense of Father Carmody's former eminence on campus and treated him accordingly.

"Courvoisier, Murph. In a snifter."

Murph looked mournfully at Roger, expecting, and getting, his request for a Diet Coke.

"What do you want to know, Roger?"

"Tell me the details about his disappearance. The newspaper accounts raise so many questions, and of course Brother Joachim's story raises more."

Father Carmody shrugged that off. "There's little to tell. He was carousing with fellow students in downtown South Bend, left early and alone, and was never seen again."

"Except by Pelligrino."

"The story? It's fiction, Roger."

"What efforts were made to find him?"

"If money could have done it he would have been found. I tried to persuade his aunt that the expenditure was pointless."

"Pointless."

"The boy was dead. I was certain of that from the beginning."

"Why?"

"Why was I certain? Experience. We have, thank God, had few such instances, but disappearances were always resolved by dissipation, accident, whatever, but almost always death. It is not easy for somebody to become nobody."

"So the search was ended."

"Eventually."

"What family was there?"

"Of the Quinns? Innumerable, if you spread wide enough a net. None, if you mean immediate. The aunt who survived him."

"What was she like?"

Father Carmody inhaled the vapors from the snifter that Murph had placed before him and smiled. "You assume I knew her."

"Didn't you?"

"Yes. Her husband and I were in the seminary together."

"The seminary!"

"Oh, he was never ordained, Gerry Quinn. Sometimes I think he was too good to be a priest. Don't quote me. In a seminary, a man who scrupulously keeps the rule is an oddball. A holy oddball. His very conscientiousness tells against him. Not that anyone would question a man's vocation because he was faithful to the rule. It doesn't work that way. In any case, he was let go. He took tonsure and some minor orders, and that was that."

"What did he do when he left the seminary?"

"Married a wife and lived happily ever after. He was dead when his nephew disappeared, but the widow was devoted to Timothy."

"And spared no expense to find her disappeared nephew."

"It was as if her purpose in life had been torn from her."

"What about the girl, Beth Hanrahan?"

"A saint." Father Carmody sipped his brandy. "An uncomfortable saint. Do you know of Dorothy Day?"

Roger nodded.

"Like that. Not a barrel of laughs, but good as gold."

Father Carmody's effort to think the story Joachim had sent was pure fiction seemed a willing suspension of belief. Joachim had used the actual names of himself and his friends.

Two days later, a sheet of paper was slipped under the doors of three offices in Brownson. Roger read his with a tolerant smile.

> *An Ancient Poet*
> *New to Me*
> *And why should I have known him?*
> *X as in Unknown was He*
> *Intent to Read the Universe*
> *Matter and All the Rest,*
> *Encoded His Thought in Verse*
> *Numbered Lines His Sly Bequest*
> *Each Can Read Them as He Will*
> *Some with a Special Skill.*

14　MAME CHILDERS, NÉE SAYERS, LIVED in an apartment on the Upper East Side that occupied the entire twelfth floor. Huge. A wonderful place in which to entertain, dinners, cocktail parities, informal little seminars with artists, writers, politicians. Financial advisers. She threw back her head and directed smoke at the ceiling. When she bent over an ashtray to stub out her cigarette, her eyes went around the vast, beautifully furnished living room. Not much of a view, unless you liked reservoirs and the endless construction work on the Museum of Modern Art. She didn't have to close her eyes to imagine Dave Williams on his feet before that bookcase, speaking with quiet authority to the half-dozen people she had gathered to hear him. How possessive she had felt. And with good reason.

"Who advises you now?" he had asked her over lunch the first time they had seen one another since South Bend. Mame felt she was recapturing an earlier role.

She liked the way he frowned when she told him she had left things in the hands of Wilfrid's advisers.

"Wilfrid?"

"My husband."

"I'm sorry."

"For what?"

"When did he . . ." His expression finished the question.

"Dave, he's not dead. We're divorced. And still friends. More or less."

She had resolved to get that on the table right away, and she was prepared for the reaction he tried to hide. In the world in which they had been raised, divorce and marriage did not go together like a horse and carriage.

"You're saying he still handles your money."

"Not personally, but I stayed with the same group after things were divided up."

If she had resolved to ease into full disclosure about her marital status, she parceled out information about how much she had emerged with from her marriage. Wilfrid had been generous, but then he was the libertine. Running around was one thing—she supposed most men were unable to say no—but for Wilfrid to have stashed a mistress two streets away verged on contempt. It was odd that their divorce had given Wilfrid an excuse to disencumber himself of all his romantic chains. Whenever they met he wore a penitent's smile.

"I don't blame you," he said.

"Blame me!"

"I gave you cause. All that's over now, you know."

"Oh, for heaven's sake."

Wilfrid had loved to have her talk about her Catholic girlhood, of graduating from St. Mary's College. City boy that he was, he thought that the college's location in Indiana would be as exotic as the fact that it was Catholic. How few native New Yorkers there are, though, and they have to come from somewhere, and why not from Indiana?

"An all-women's college?"

"Across the road from Notre Dame."

She had trilled on about the wonderful odds for a St. Mary's girl with the seven-to-one ratio of male to female.

"Even so, you didn't marry one."

"He got away."

Little bleats of incredulity whenever she mentioned this. Mame Childers not getting anything she wanted? Impossible. It became a line in her standard repertoire. Repetition altered her memory of those days, and she could half believe that it was she rather than Beth Hanrahan who had been such a great hit on the campus across the road. Of course, Beth had been an actress, on and off the stage, and her role from junior year on had been that of the perplexed Venus trying to decide between vying suitors. Dave Williams had been one of them. Mame had actually thought, *If Beth discards Dave, he's mine.* Seconds.

Dave Williams had to think, or maybe that was a pretense, when Mame mentioned Beth Hanrahan.

"David, she was wild about you. Of course, we all were."

How manipulable men are, particularly hardheaded practical men. Take them away from business and they were like boys again.

So it had begun, a Manhattan romance, plays, concerts, eating out, talking, talking. Well, Dave talking. Silence, a listening silence, is the great seducer.

She explained why Wilfrid didn't matter. "We were never really married, Dave. Not in our sense."

"Will you marry again?"

"I haven't been asked."

Bold that, but he was remembering something. He had it. "Dr. Johnson said that to marry again is the triumph of hope over experience."

"What did he know?"

"Well, he didn't marry again after his wife died."

An observation, a policy statement, a muted warning off? Mame couldn't tell.

"How much you know, Dave."

"Notre Dame '89."

She put her hand on his. "St. Mary's '89."

It might have been a ceremony. That night he came home with her. "Mame," he began, when they were in the elevator. She put her fingers on his lips. He kissed them away. Later he said, "I don't go to bed with all my clients."

"Is that how you think of me, a client?"

Still later, looking at him asleep beside her, she thought, well, it had taken time, but at last she had edged out Beth Hanrahan.

"Where did you live when you were married?" he asked at breakfast.

"Here."

He just looked at her. Was he thinking that he had taken Wilfrid's place, in the same bed . . . No one else had ever done that. Her few lapses had been in far-off places where they hadn't seemed to count. It was a mistake to bring him here. She saw that now. Dear God, what would Wilfrid think?

"I spent a year redecorating," she lied.

It hadn't helped. Maybe in "their" sense she had never really been married, but he had the look of an adulterer, not a lover. She never made that mistake again. She began to speak of putting the apartment on the market.

"You'd just have to buy another."

"Maybe I would settle down in the place in Connecticut."

The next time they went there, but it was almost as bad. The one thing Wilfrid had resisted, unsuccessfully, was letting her have the place in Connecticut. It had been far more his than theirs. He had spent weekends doing maintenance, fussing around the property, directing old Fitz as the grumbling caretaker trimmed trees, made flower beds, painted the little cabin that had been Mame's special place. It was fifty yards from the main house, reached by a wonderful little winding path, emerging suddenly like something in a fairy tale. Dave loved her office there. How delighted he had been to see so many of Casey's books on her shelves.

"Are you still in touch with him, Dave?"

"He's become a recluse on Siesta Key. He and Peaches."

"Peaches!"

"His wife. Much younger. I have a place on Longboat."

She had stayed at the Longboat Key Club, which, he told her, was not a mile from his place.

"I'd love to see it," she said.

They did spend some wonderful days on Longboat Key. It had the added attraction of being far from Manhattan, and Wilfrid.

"Why don't we call Casey?" she said one day.

"Another time."

She seemed to be his secret, which had its attractions. On the other hand, it suggested that he was not comfortable in their relationship.

"You should marry again," she said boldly, busying herself tidying up while she said it.

Silence. It had been three years since his wife, Bridget, had died. He never talked about her. Sometimes Mame felt that Bridget was the one he didn't want to know about them. It was going to take time, she could see that, but she could be patient.

Meanwhile, he did wonders with the money she entrusted to him. Did he think it was everything? Wilfrid hadn't liked it when she said she wanted to move some money into David Williams's care.

"Never heard of him."

"We were in school together."

Jason, his partner, had heard of Dave. So had Pincus, their common financial adviser.

"A good man. He's doing very well." Pincus brightened. "You put that amount with him and we'll have a contest to see who's the better adviser."

That made it sound like a game. Then again, what else is investing?

"He's an old friend. From college."

Pincus didn't like that. "Never do business with friends."

She put her hand on his arm. "I thought you loved me."

"Not while I'm handling your money."

It seemed disloyal, letting Pincus see the reports Dave sent her. He wrinkled his nose. "He's beating me. Not that I would put you into some of these things. Hedge funds are pretty volatile."

Hedge funds. It sounded like an item in the Connecticut place budget. Dave had tried to explain them to her, seeking her go-ahead.

"David, I am in your hands." She leaned toward him and kissed the tip of his nose.

Many of the investments Dave had made for her turned out to be volatile. To his credit, Pincus hadn't crowed when Dave's reports began to detail losses.

"Temporary," he assured her. "The market is adjusting itself."

Bad financial news had seemed a good time to bring things out into the open.

"It's been over a year, Dave."

"What?"

"Us."

She waited. He looked away.

"Is that your answer?"

"What's the question?"

"The one a man puts to a woman."

"Mame, you're divorced."

She dropped her chin and looked at him over her half-glasses. "You know I was never really married."

He looked at her for a moment. "I talked with a priest about that."

"You did!"

"Father Carmody, at Notre Dame. A nonsacramental marriage can be a real marriage."

"That's his opinion?"

"Yes."

"Why did you ask him?"

It was his turn to tuck in his chin.

"I want another opinion, Dave."

She got it from a fussy monsignor in a church near Sutton Place. He called it the Church of the United Nations and was full of stories about important people who showed up for Mass.

"No problem, my dear," he assured Mame when she explained her situation.

"You're sure? The man has been told otherwise."

Monsignor Sparrow was incensed. "I serve on the archdiocesan marriage court."

"We could be married here?"

That raised the delicate matter of her nonattendance at Mass. She couldn't remember the last time she had gone to confession. So she told him about St. Mary's and Notre Dame and her civil marriage and how she and Dave had been students together. "This is my chance to get back on track, Monsignor."

"Good. Good."

Only it was bad, bad. Dave wasn't going to let a New York monsignor second-guess his precious Father Carmody.

There was more.

"Mame, I never proposed."

"I'm just a hot little affair?"

"It's over, Mame. It has to be. I can't keep confessing the same sin over and over and pretend I'm truly sorry."

"Sin!"

He meant it. All those wonderful times meant only sin to him.

"It doesn't have to be a sin." Did she have to come right out and say it? *Marry me and everything is fine. A sin becomes a virtue.*

"Please don't laugh, Mame, but I still feel married. I think of Bridget all the time."

"All the time?" She widened her eyes.

At first, calmly, she had described him to himself. A member of the archdiocesan marriage court of New York had told her there was no impediment to her marrying again, but Dave stuck with an off-the-cuff remark of an old priest at Notre Dame. Didn't he see that their love was a prelude to something permanent, not an affair? A pardonable anticipation.

"Did the monsignor tell you that, too?"

She remained calm. "I admire and respect your devotion to Bridget, but Dave, she's not your wife anymore. Until death do us part, remember? Don't turn what I am sure are wonderful memories into an impediment to future happiness."

It was an argument she was bound to lose, because such things are never settled by arguments. What had been hesitation, reluctance, became coldness. They saw one another less. Meanwhile, the money she had entrusted to him was melting away. Pincus urged her to pull out. He was riding out the meltdown pretty well. However, she had decided something she would never express to Pincus. She wanted David to go smash, lose all her money, hit bottom, become vulnerable again. She sent him an e-mail saying that Larry Briggs was urging her and several of those she had directed to him to consider a class action suit. Dave was still falling, not yet at rock bottom.

She had contacted Casey Winthrop on her own, invoking old times and telling him how much she enjoyed reading him. On a trip to Florida, she visited him and Peaches. She didn't mention David Williams. His name came up later when Peaches attached to an e-mail the notice that Dave's place on Longboat Key was on the market.

"If it drops another hundred thousand, I may make a bid."

When Larry Briggs called, asking if she knew where in the world Dave Williams was, Mame was almost flattered that she should be expected to know.

"Get him on his cell phone."

"I want to speak to him face-to-face."

"I know the feeling. He could be in Florida. He has a condo on Longboat Key and a classmate on Siesta Key."

"What's his name?"

"Casey Winthrop. Would you like his number?"

"How much did he lose for you?"

"The market will come back."

Briggs tried to laugh, unsuccessfully. Mame had half a mind to call Flip and tell her to keep her husband away from windows in high buildings.

(15) EMIL CHADWICK HAD A LITTLE house—they called it a villa for reasons into which he did not probe—in Holy Cross Village, across Highway 31 from the campus. He had joined the Notre Dame faculty in 1955, a fact that sometimes surprised even himself. Not that he had come here, but that it was so long ago.

Once he'd had a wife, but those married years were sandwiched between long pre and post stretches until he could almost believe that he had always been a bachelor. Almost. He still dreamt of Maude; he talked to her all the time, out loud, why not? He lived alone. The house in which he and Maude raised the kids had seemed haunted after she died. Not that he minded the ghosts. It was no place in which to live alone. Even so, he hung in there until five years ago when he had been offered his villa and took it almost without forethought, as if it were his destiny. He brought his ghosts along. "This is my final address," he would say, sometimes in company. When he went gaga, they could just roll him down the road and put him in the special care unit.

It was called a retirement village. That meant they had all come here to die.

"Like Holy Cross House," Father Carmody said cheerily.

"I never thought you would go there, Father."

"I am in the place but not of it."

It was the vanity of age to think that one was not like the rest of men. Chadwick felt the same way in the village. He seldom ate with the others, although there was a choice of restaurants. The food was fine, but the company . . . Those who had come into the village after he did were required to take so many meals a month, but Chadwick was free of that, thank God. It was amazing what one could do with a microwave. He had been fending for himself since Maude died, so that wasn't much of a change.

"You've been grandfathered," Carmody said.

"In every sense of the term."

He had three grandchildren. One son was a seminary professor, a layman who had thought he had a vocation and, when that proved not to be the case, stayed on as a member of the faculty. Emil couldn't understand why Nick did not go on to ordination. Carmody had talked with Nick about it. "Scruples," Carmody said to Emil. Maurice, his oldest, was a monk in Kentucky, a Trappist. He figured the kids had got religion from their mother, who had converted when they married and acquired the zeal of a convert. Maggie lived with her family in Portland. She called him once a week, but it was a long trip from Oregon, and he seldom saw her or her husband, Bill, or the children.

Roger Knight had seemed surprised when Emil first mentioned his children. Well, only old-timers like Carmody would remember Maude. Sometimes he strolled around Cedar Grove Cemetery, on Notre Dame Avenue, going from grave to grave, conducting a posthumous faculty meeting. He had not thought death had undone so many. All of his contemporaries lay there, as did Maude, with a place beside her reserved for him. His name was on the stone next to hers, with only his birth date. February 9, 1931. Colleagues who weren't buried in Cedar Grove, those who were members of the

Congregation of Holy Cross, were buried in the community ceme-tery, which was on the road that led to St. Mary's. Most of the priests lying there had died since Emil joined the faculty. He would pedal out there on his three-wheeled cycle, stand at the south end, where Father Sorin's grave was, and look out over the rows and rows of identical white crosses. Keats was hardly more than a boy when he fell half in love with easeful death. Chadwick knew the feeling.

An old man is a bundle of memories, and it was a pleasure to just sit still and let them come. No need to stir them up; they always seemed to be waiting for him. At night, he would often put down his book, turn off the lights, and sit on in the dark, remembering. In his Brownson office, a favorite book could induce long thoughts, and he would lay it open on his chest, close his eyes, and just think. When the first message came, he had been undisturbed by the whispering in the hall. When the sheet came under his door, he ignored it. Doubtless more administrative nonsense. He had turned in his chair to see the couple leave the building.

The second message had come at night when he was meditating in his unlit office. Napping actually, but that was all right. Had he been wakened by the sound in the hall? The light beneath the door was broken and a sheet slipped under. He had turned in his chair and looked out toward the parking lot, and then a young man came into the light before hurrying away.

He hadn't mentioned those kids when he and Roger and Sarah had talked about the messages. *Your days are numbered.* He might have sent the message to himself. Once he had read a novel in which a character composed fortune cookie messages for herself, allowing a sufficient gap between composition and reading to ensure surprise.

He sat on for half an hour before turning on his desk lamp and fetching the sheet of paper. Dear God, what a dreadful poem.

They discussed it the following day, he and Sarah and Roger. Sarah professed to be upset, but then she was an excitable young lady. One of his few informants left in her department had assured Chadwick that Sarah would be offered the tenured position. Chadwick had been sworn to secrecy, of course, but he knew all about academic secrecy. Sarah was convinced that the flat tires and Emil's bicycle pump were part of the campaign to drive her crazy.

"Why is one driven crazy? I always preferred walking."

She was not to be diverted. Roger, to Emil's surprise, agreed with her that the flat tires were integral to the plot. "It's plain as a pikestaff."

Emil threw up his hands and roared with delight. They were still discussing the ways in which a pikestaff was plain when Sarah left them in disgust.

"I saw the boy who left that poem, Roger."

"I think I know who he is."

"There was a girl with him the first time."

"Not the second?"

"No."

"Good."

"I'M A FRIEND OF YOUR FATHER'S," the voice on the phone said. It was midmorning; Jay had been sleeping in and resented the ringing of the phone. "Larry Briggs. Perhaps he's mentioned me."

"Maybe. I'm not sure."

"Is he still on campus?"

Jay sat up in bed and opened his eyes. Until he did that, he had been hoping he could just fall back and into sleep again. He told Larry Briggs that his father had flown out yesterday.

"Damn."

"I can give you his cell phone number."

"I have that!"

"Well . . ."

"I'd like to talk with you."

"Okay."

"I meant face-to-face. How about lunch?"

Geez. "Were you a classmate of Dad's?"

"Almost."

They met in the student center, where there were four choices of cholesterol. Briggs stood out like a figure in one of the old pictures of Notre Dame. He was stoop-shouldered as if he had just put down the globe and hadn't straightened up yet. Funny-looking suit, wild tie, a lean and hungry look. After shaking hands, they got into line and moved along until they ordered.

"What noise," Briggs said as they waited for their orders to appear.

It was noisy. Jay had stopped noticing.

They found a table, and Briggs looked at the contents of his tray. He plucked a french fry from the little bag. "I'm a client of your father's."

Jay nodded and took a bite of his burger.

"I've lost a lot of money."

"I'm sorry."

"I trusted him. We all trusted him." Briggs picked up another french fry and flourished it as if he were directing the Ronald McDonald band.

Jay didn't know what to say. "You came out here to see him?"

"I think he's dodging me. Mame Childers is protecting him."

"Who is Mame Childers?"

Briggs looked as if he were about to say something, then waved away the question.

Jay sat back. Briggs looked a little spacey to him. Large tragic eyes, his nose crooked, his mouth working as if he were eating, which he wasn't. Jay got out his phone. "I'll see if I can get hold of him."

"No! Don't do that. I want to surprise him."

Surprise him? Why should a client be a surprise? Jay punched the number anyway. His father answered after three rings.

"Dad, a man named Larry Briggs is here on campus. He came here hoping to see you. What's it all about?"

Briggs followed what Jay was saying, his hands opening and closing.

"He's there?"

"Sitting across the table from me."

"Let me talk to him."

Jay handed the phone across the table, but Briggs backed away from it, shaking his head. What a weirdo Briggs was. He reminded Jay of a lurking figure in a horror movie, the secret sharer, put off by everyone and everything.

"He doesn't want to talk on the phone, Dad."

A longish silence. "Tell him I will expect to see him at my office."

"Is that where you are?"

"I will be by the time he gets back."

Briggs got to his feet when Jay snapped his phone shut. Jay gave him the message.

"Did he say where he is?"

Jay was liking this less and less. "He said to meet him at his office."

Briggs stared down at Jay. His long-fingered hands closed on the back of his chair. "Your father's son," he said.

"What's that supposed to mean?"

Briggs just shook his head, then picked up the little sack of french fries and took it with him as he wound his way among the tables to the door.

Jay put through another call to his father. "He's gone."

"I'm sorry he bothered you, Jay. He's pretty upset by what the market has been doing."

"He's a nut."

A chuckle. "You may be right."

"Who is Mame Childers?"

A pause. "Another client."

"Dad, I'd watch out for that guy Briggs."

17 ——————➤ "I DON'T KNOW WHAT YOU'RE TALK-
ing about," Jay Williams said when Roger
told him he had received his poem.

"I won't say that I enjoyed it as poetry, but as a code, it is interesting."

Jay sat forward with the beginning of a smile on his face.

"The initial letters," Roger said.

Jay fell back, shaking his head. "Congratulations. You really are
a detective."

"Oh, anybody could have figured this out. Anyone who had the
air let out of his tires, that is."

The initial letters spelled Anaximenes, the pre-Socratic philosopher who thought he could reduce the variety of things to their elements and the other elements to air.

"So what was the point, Jay?"

"I was testing your detective skills." The little smile was gone,
replaced by an apparently sincere expression of concern. "You've
met my father."

"Yes."

"He's in trouble."

"What kind of trouble?"

"I don't know. This financial mess has hit him hard, I know that.

If he wasn't my father, I would think the recession was divine justice. I think there's something more, though."

"Why don't you ask him?"

"Would you want to quiz your father?"

Roger wondered if David Williams would want to tell his son about the strange bequest from his old classmate, Brother Joachim. On the other hand, why should that be kept a secret from his son? The surprising bonanza would surely go a long way toward solving any financial difficulties David Williams was in, but his impulsive, almost horrified statement that he would have nothing to do with the money seemed connected with the confessional story Brother Joachim had sent to the archives. That didn't seem to be it, though.

"One of his clients was out here and wanted to see me. A man named Briggs. A spooky guy."

"Spooky?"

"He all but threatened my father."

"You should tell your father."

"I did." Jay inhaled. "What are your rates?"

"How do you mean?"

"I want to hire a detective."

"You couldn't afford me."

"Oh, but I could. I'm loaded, thanks to my mother."

Roger Knight said nothing.

"The client who looked me up? Larry Briggs. I think he is stalking my father."

Roger listened to the account of Briggs's visit. "Just french fries?"

"I ate his cheeseburger after he left."

"I think I know what's bothering your father, Jay."

"What?"

"He will tell you if he wants you to know."

"What's the big secret?"

"Is it a secret just because he hasn't told you?"

"You ought to write poetry."

"Oh, I do."

Jay left, angry. All students have rough edges—how could they not, given their age?—but Jay Williams was difficult to like. Amanda, of course, was another story.

"Jay told me about that stupid poem, Professor. And letting the air out of your tires. I had nothing to do with that."

"I never thought you did."

Emil Chadwick made a face when Roger tracked down the initial letters of the poem that had been slipped under their doors. "There's a name for that sort of thing."

"Anaximenes."

"Usually the initial letters give the name of the dedicatee, Roger. Maybe no one could write a decent poem under those constraints."

"I've explained it to Sarah, so she will know that her receiving copies of the messages had no more to do with her than it did with you."

Chadwick mumbled once again through Jay Williams's coded verse. "Do you know what Johnson said of Pope's *Essay on Man*?"

"Tell me."

"I'll do better. I'll read it to you." He rolled toward a bookshelf and ran his finger over his complete set of Samuel Johnson. Having found *The Lives of the Poets*, he opened it and, after a moment, read. "'The subject is perhaps not very proper for poetry, and the poet was not sufficiently master of his subject; metaphysical morality was to him a new study, he was proud of his acquisitions, and, supposing himself master of great secrets, was in haste to teach what he had not learned.'"

He clapped the book shut and beamed at Roger.

"Wonderful," Roger agreed.

"He goes on and on like that. Of course, he liked most of Pope."

"And Dryden."

"Yes. He places those two above all the others he treated. And both were Catholic."

The thought of giving a seminar on Dryden and Pope drifted across Roger's mind, but another thought was more insistent. "Your son is a Trappist monk."

"In Kentucky."

"Do you ever visit him?"

Chadwick looked abject. "You have touched on a sore point. He is geographically closer than my other children—it is only a half day's drive to Gethsemani Abbey—yet it has been three years since I was there."

"We ought to pay him a visit sometime."

"Are you serious?"

"Midsemester could be a possibility."

Chadwick became almost excited. "We could stay in the guesthouse."

"You're able to talk with your son?"

"Trappist silence? A thing of the past. One of Maurice's complaints."

"There's another monk there I'd like to see."

Jay Williams, who had acquired a stringent view on usury, thought the financial crisis was divine justice. He also thought his father was in danger from some of his clients. His father's reaction to the bequest from Brother Joachim suggested that there was another sort of retribution troubling David Williams. Was Brother Joachim engaged in some sort of celestial blackmail? Roger was eager to talk to the monk, but there were weeks to go before he could set off with Emil Chadwick for Our Lady of Gethsemani monastery in Kentucky. Meanwhile Phil had grown impatient of all the mystery.

"Jimmy Stewart and I are going to move that rock and dig to see if there is anything there."

"So you've told Jimmy." Stewart was a detective on the South Bend police with whom they had struck up a friendship. "Have you told Father Carmody what you intend to do?"

"He'll be there."

So early one morning a small band left the road beneath the Log Chapel and trudged across the lawn to the boulder. Father Carmody grunted beside Roger as they followed Phil and Jimmy Stewart, who were armed with a pickaxe and a shovel, respectively. In the first light, the campus had an odd allure, waiting for sun to bring it into its full beauty.

"I feel like a grave robber," Roger said.

"Let's see what we find."

Even a small boulder is a boulder, and this one had settled into the ground over the years since Patrick Pelligrino had placed it as the marker for the spot where he claimed to have buried the body of Timothy Quinn. Jimmy got one point of the pickaxe under the boulder, jiggling it down, until it served as a lever. He leaned on the handle, and the boulder moved. Phil shoved his spade under the opening. Jimmy's next effort got the boulder on end, and with his foot he toppled it free. Then Phil went to work, making a neat pile of the dirt he removed. The others stood around, watching expectantly.

The rotted box was three feet down. Jimmy and Phil crouched over the hole while Roger and Father Carmody kibitzed over their shoulders.

"I don't see any bones," Father Carmody said. He sounded relieved.

With the shovel, Phil knocked away the rotted wood and reached into the hole. Then he stopped, put on his glove, and reached again. The morning sun had begun to slant through the trees when he brought forth what had been beside the box. They all stared at it.

A hatchet.

"Is that all?"

"He only buried the hatchet," Father Carmody cried, relishing the phrase.

No, there was more. Roger lumbered forward and lowered himself to his knees. He lifted a side of the box that had crumbled. He let out an enormous sigh and gestured to Father Carmody.

"What is it?" the priest asked, bending down next to Roger.

"Bones, Father."

"Dear God." Father Carmody's hand went up, and he traced a blessing over the remains.

"Those aren't the bones of an adult," Roger said.

Father Carmody said nothing.

PART TWO

THE BODY IN
THE HERMITAGE

1 DAVE HAD DELLA SET UP AN AP-
pointment for Larry Briggs, and Larry was
there half an hour early. When he was ready for him, Dave went to
the room in which Della had put him to find Larry glaring at the
numbers flickering across the screen.

"I hate those goddam things."

"Actually it's the best day we've had in weeks."

"Meaning lousy."

"Let's go to my office."

"What's wrong with here?"

"Not a thing. Larry, I've wanted to have this conversation for a
long time."

"Then why have you been dodging me? I flew out to Notre Dame,
hoping to catch you there, but you were already gone."

"I won't have you bothering my son, Larry."

"It's you I want to bother. Your secretary told me—"

"Administrative assistant," Dave corrected.

"Whatever. She told me you were in Florida, but you were gone
by the time I got there."

"I wasn't at my condo on Longboat Key."

"I went to Siesta Key."

"Casey Winthrop?"

"That's right."

Dave already knew of this because Casey had called to ask if his other clients were as nutty as Briggs.

"Why else would they be my clients?"

"Mame isn't nutty."

"No." That was when Dave had decided to unload Larry Briggs.

"I'm sorry you went to all that pointless trouble, Larry."

"Pointless! Do you know what this is doing to Philippa? As you damned well know, that money came from the sale of her father's business."

"Larry, my suggestion is that you get out of the market."

"You're dropping me?" Larry was aghast.

"You don't have the temperament for it. Let's cash you out—"

"What could I possibly gain by that? Last time we talked, you sounded optimistic."

"I think the market will correct itself, yes. In time. But it will take more patience than you've got."

"Bullshit." Briggs sat up as he said this, then once more slumped forward, his menacing hands dangling between his knees. He looked as if he'd like to put them around Dave's throat. "You've put me in the poorhouse." Now he sounded like he was going to cry.

"Not quite that bad. Larry, here is my proposal. We will cash you out, and I will make up the difference between what we realize and your original investment."

Larry turned his head and stared at Dave. He began to nod. "That's what I want, all right, but not that way. You're as bad as Bernie Madoff. I'm going to sue."

"You'd lose and waste a lot of money besides."

"I want people to know what you've done to me."

"Any lawyer, well, almost any lawyer, would advise against that."

"You're worried about the publicity."

"Well, I wouldn't welcome it. Let's do what I suggested. I hope you understand that I am under no obligation to do what I propose."

"I don't want your charity."

"Just my scalp?"

"Yes!"

Dave observed some moments of silence. He decided not to tell Larry again what he thought of his bothering Jay with his problems. "Larry, today would be a good day for you to get out. Let's look into it."

They moved to Dave's office; he called in Della and told her that Larry was cashing out.

"Just tell me what I'm worth now."

"That's what we're going to do."

Half an hour later, Della brought him the figures. Dave glanced at them and tried not to think how much he would have to add to the amount on the basis of the proposal he had made to Larry. He handed Larry the paper.

"My God!"

"Shall I sell?" Della asked.

"Larry?"

"You meant what you said earlier?"

"Yes."

"You're trying to buy me off."

"Larry, you're a hard guy to be nice to."

Larry glared at Della. "Sell it all."

Dave nodded, and Della withdrew.

Larry was staring at the figures he had been given. "I've lost at least forty percent."

"That leaves you quite a bit. Bank it, Larry. Bank it and forget about it."

"Don't think this squares us, Dave. Maybe I can find an adviser who knows what he's doing."

For the rest of the week, the market was on a sharply rising line.

Larry called, furious. "You sonofabitch."

"Larry, you haven't lost or gained a thing. You're back where you were."

"After what you've put me through?"

He slammed down the phone.

2 AFTER PEACHES TOLD CASEY OF MAME
Childers's interest in Dave Williams's place on Longboat Key, she fell silent, a little kewpie doll smile on her lips, eyes wide.

"Why would she want a place on Longboat Key?"

"She doesn't."

"So you don't think she's serious?"

"You tell me. She's your friend. Know what I do think?"

What Peaches thought was that Mame would like to buy the place and sign it back to Dave Williams. "Casey, he's all she talks about. She's nuts about him."

He thought about that. She had been nuts about Dave years ago, when they were all students. Casey knew that because he had become her target of opportunity, her ticket into all their doings; no member of the trinity would ask her.

"They had girls of their own?"

"The same one. Beth Hanrahan."

"They couldn't all take out the same girl!"

"It all depends what you mean by taking out. We did things together. Pat wrote plays, Beth and Dave starred in them, Quinn was a poet."

"And you?"

"I wrote sports for the *Observer*."

She leaned over him and kissed his nose. "I love you."

She crossed the room and eased herself into a chair, sighing as she did so. The phrase "heavy with child" turned out not to be a metaphor. "So who was Mame's boyfriend?"

"Me."

"I take back that kiss."

Memories of Notre Dame and of his classmates, particularly the trinity and Beth and Mame, began to interfere with the plot of the novel he was writing. He tried to banish them by making notes, but that only increased the flow of memories and, more to the point, thoughts of what he could make of them, fictionwise. Isn't that what Pat had attempted in the story he sent to the archives? Casey was powerfully tempted to set aside the novel he was working on and give full attention to what was now a distraction. In a later preface to *Ethan Frome*, Edith Wharton had mentioned the temptation a writer often feels when, in the midst of one story, an idea for another occurs, one which always looks more alluring than the one being written. Her advice: Never succumb to that temptation. Finish what you have started before turning to anything else. It was advice that Casey had always followed even if, as he learned, Edith Wharton hadn't. She was forever setting things aside in favor of another story. Maybe her fervor in that preface was the plea of the fallen rather than the stern voice of discipline.

Casey set aside the Western he was writing, looked at the notes he had taken while fighting temptation, threw them away, and started as he always had, by starting. He would discover the story as he went along. Maybe that's what Pat Pelligrino had done when writing the story he sent to the Notre Dame archives. Dave, when he told Casey about it, tried to laugh it off, but it was clear it bothered him. No wonder. Joachim all but accused him of taking a hatchet to

Timothy Quinn. Casey was sure he could make a better story of those events.

Three guys after the same girl, and one of them disappears. The other two look accusingly at one another. The story would bring out the fact that each had reason to suspect that the other had something to do with the missing member of the trinity. The disappearance alters the chemistry of the group, as Timothy Quinn's disappearance had affected them all. The girl becomes wrapped up in things at St. Mary's. Pat stops writing, Dave switches his major to business, and nothing is what it was before. Except Casey and Mame. They lasted right up to graduation, almost beyond it, but Casey briefly took a job on the sports page of the Sioux City paper, and Mame went to New York.

For years, nothing, and now Dave with his business apparently gone belly up wants to liquidate his Florida holdings. He came down again for the sale of his boat, and they had lunch at Marina Jack's to celebrate the price the boat had brought. Of course, it was sad the boat had to go.

"You can always buy another."

"I've been thinking of how seldom we used that one."

"Mame Childers paid us a visit."

"She's a client of mine."

"So she said. Is she as loaded as she appears?"

"She came out of her divorce with a pile."

"Divorce?"

"She was married to a non-Catholic."

"How do people live in Manhattan?"

Dave thought about it. "From day to day. Like everywhere else."

Casey thought of Larry Briggs. What a business Dave was in. And Casey had thought editors were a pain in the posterior.

He said, "Mame seems interested in this area."

Dave just nodded.

"She's asked Peaches about your place on Longboat."

"Come on."

"Scout's honor."

"She's lost a lot of money lately. Thanks to me."

"She doesn't act like it." A boat went past the deck on which they sat and headed into the Gulf. "What a contrast to Beth Hanrahan?"

"Her model is Dorothy Day."

Casey sipped his beer, thinking of his plot. "You and Mame are the only ones I've seen. Of course, I'm a kind of recluse, as Peaches keeps reminding me."

"You've got a good life. Not long ago, at a rental car counter, I noticed that the clerk was reading one of your books."

"Good for her. How about you? Have you ever visited Pat?"

"Our Trappist classmate? I've been thinking about it." He seemed to be thinking about it then. "He left me some money."

"Where does a monk get money?"

"It was an inheritance. He left it all to me before he entered."

"Lucky you."

"But why me?"

"Who else is there?"

"You."

"Dave, I was never a member of the trinity, and he couldn't very well leave it to Tim."

"How can anyone just disappear, Casey? One day he's walking around campus like everyone else, and the next day, pfft. He's gone."

"A dead body disappears in a relatively short time."

"Until it does, it has to be somewhere."

Both lakes on campus had been dragged, and even when the searches proved futile, it was thought the body would surface sooner or later. It never had. The river hadn't delivered up a body either, but how can you drag a whole river? Those searches were based on the hunch that Tim had drowned himself. Committed suicide. Beth would have been the motive. He was sure that Dave was her choice. Pat had thought the same. The crack-up had begun. Wherever Tim went he must have walked. He hadn't flown out of South Bend; he hadn't taken the South Shore to Chicago, or the airport limousine.

"Hitchhike," Casey said. "Someone gives a kid a lift and never connects that to any stories about a missing Notre Dame student, if he even saw them. There are lots of ways."

"You think he's still alive?"

"It's a helluva story, Dave. It would make a novel."

"You going to do that?"

"I'll change the names to protect the innocent."

"That's ghoulish."

"Dave, that's what stories do, make sense out of what in reality is mystifying."

"How's your Western going?"

"The way of all flesh."

"In a Western?"

"You'd be surprised."

3 WHEN BETH HANRAHAN HAD RENTED
the studio on Franklin Avenue years ago, her
parents and siblings had thought she was nuts, and they had a case.
The area had been on the decline for years; it wasn't a safe place for
a young woman just out of college to live, but as soon as she saw
the large area of the studio and the huge slanted windows giving her
a more or less northern light, the die was cast. Days, she worked
downtown in an advertising agency, one of half a dozen artists
whose talents were turned to enticing consumers into buying more
or less useless things. The pay was good, and Beth saved most of
what she earned and consoled herself with the thought that the Anderson Agency was merely a means to support her dream of becoming an artist.

Ever since graduation she had seemed to drift. Listening to the
rhetoric of the commencement speaker, she realized that she didn't
feel at all on the threshold of an exciting future. There had been the
disappearance of Timothy and her knowledge of what had precipi-
tated it. She felt that her life had ended rather than that it was about
to begin. Art had seemed a way out of the doldrums.

Where had that dream come from? She had always drawn; she
loved the feel of soft lead on thick paper seeming to move her hand
along rather than vice versa. She had never had an art lesson. In her
senior year at St. Mary's she had gone once to an art class with Mame,

caught up in one of her temporary enthusiasms, but Beth decided she did not need the spur of a class in order to train herself. It was the woodcuts in the *Catholic Worker* that intrigued her and anything by Ada Bethune, then a hot ticket in liturgical art. She had tried that for a while, designing cards for the Liturgical Press in Collegeville, but all her stuff was derivative, more of what already existed. She liked pastels and watercolors but dreaded working with oils. She was an apprentice, wondering what her medium would be, what her subjects.

The dream of being an artist had suffered from those dreadful events in senior year, but slowly it had revived when she was back in Minneapolis.

"Where did you go to art school?" she would be asked at Anderson's when they had left their boards for a cup of coffee.

"I didn't."

"How on earth did you get a job here?"

"I brought a portfolio of things."

"Who didn't? I thought you had to have gone to Walker or wherever to get in here."

"It never came up."

That was Jane, who had become a friend. Unfortunately, Jane had taken on the myth that artists, even commercial artists, were not confined by the codes that kept the lower orders in line. When Jane saw Beth's studio her first reaction was, "What a great place for a party!"

Why not? Jane arranged it. Beth didn't know a fraction of the people who crowded into her studio. There was music of a sort, far too loud, and lots to drink. Smoking, too, of several kinds.

"Isn't this wonderful?" Jane had cried, her eyes too bright, her blouse off one shoulder, but it was designed that way.

"Who are all these people?"

"Who do you want to know?" Jane's eyes widened naughtily.

Jane seemed to have put out an all points bulletin, pulling in every aspiring artist and writer on the South Side. It turned out that she and Jane were paying for the booze, hence the turnout. Her half of the bill staggered Beth.

"Jane, I can't afford to do this again."

"You won't have to. Now you'll be invited everywhere."

Invited wasn't quite the word. Announcements of parties were posted on a bulletin board at Anderson's, to whom it may concern, with the caveat that one should bring his own booze. For a time Beth got caught up in those parties that would begin on Friday night and sometimes continue into Sunday. Jane couldn't hold her liquor and became amorous, disappearing for stretches and then returning to the gaiety. Beth asked no questions, but she had her ideas. At one party Beth had a devil of a time convincing a bearded Lothario that she did not want to adjourn with him to another room. Jane came to her help, joshing the guy, telling him Beth was a nun in disguise and only liked girls. Later, Beth saw Jane adjourn with the beard.

So okay, was that what she wanted? The parties were fun, up to a point, and some of the artists were actually artists. Jane's big revelation came one evening when she asked Beth if she could come home with her. To talk.

"I'm pregnant."

"Oh, Jane."

"You're Catholic, aren't you?"

"Yes."

"So am I. A Catholic in disguise lately."

Beth dreaded where this conversation was headed. It took two hours, but finally it came. "I'm going to get an abortion." Jane seemed to be asking Beth for permission.

"Don't."

So they had that whole conversation, both of them knowing what they knew, and Jane fighting it, certain that Beth would talk differently if she were in Jane's predicament. Would she have? Maybe. God only knew. She was on the brink of telling Jane her own story but drew back. Jane could not bear to tell her parents; she was afraid that soon others at Anderson would notice.

"Take a leave, Jane. You can come up with some excuse."

"You mean, go hide somewhere and have a baby? No thanks. What would I do with it?"

"I'll take it! I'll adopt it."

It seemed to be the worst thing she could have said. Jane became furious. She stormed out of the studio and the following week missed a few days. When she came back she avoided Beth. They were never really friends again. She should have taken the occasion to confide in Jane, to let her know she understood the predicament she was in. How easily mindless passion, call it love, had the inevitable result that somehow came as a surprise. Beth brought her hands to her face, felt tears running between her fingers, and thought of her stillborn little baby of long ago.

When Beth stopped going to those wild parties, she felt a little sorry for herself, all alone in her studio while elsewhere . . . She thought of elsewhere. She thought of all the parties she had gone to. She tried to think of them as fun, but she couldn't. Suddenly it all seemed stupid. Her whole life seemed stupid. That Sunday, for the first time in weeks, she went to Mass, at Holy Rosary. Despite the usher, she managed to get a back pew. She sat during the Mass, considering the people around her, here to worship God. They seemed members of a race to which she had once belonged. She could not go to communion. When everyone went forward, pew after pew, she felt like an outcast.

She spent the afternoon brooding. Her thoughts went back to South Bend. In those days, only a few years ago then, she had been the belle of the ball, the favorite of the trinity. She smiled, remembering. Dave, Pat, and Timothy. Timothy. What a dreadful thing it had been when he disappeared. It had filled them all with dread. At first it drew them all closer together, but then it had a centrifugal effect. It was months later, back in Minneapolis, when everything seemed over, that she got the card from Timothy. He hadn't signed it, but she knew. Because of the message, some lines from John Donne. "Never send to know for whom the bell tolls; it tolls for thee." Donne had been their shared enthusiasm, hers and Tim's, especially the Holy Sonnets. The card had been mailed in San Diego. It had seemed right to consider it a secret.

The first effect of that Sunday of brooding was a resolution that she had to snap out of it.

Then she had a telephone call from Mame. "I called your parents, and they gave me your number."

"Where are you?"

"New York! Beth, I'm going to get married."

"Wonderful."

"I want you to be a bridesmaid."

How could she refuse? She didn't want to refuse. Going to a classmate's wedding seemed a return to normalcy, to the person she had been.

She went east a few days before the wedding, to try on the dress, to talk with Mame. A hectic time, but they did have several late night tête-à-têtes, long sessions of remembering South Bend. Manhattan all but overwhelmed her, and she marveled at how settled into the city Mame was. Wilfrid Childers was a bit of a surprise; he seemed years older than Mame. So was the wedding. No priest, no Mass, a generic church. One afternoon Beth had gone, all alone, to the Catholic Worker House on Mott Street.

Later, she would think that was the real reason for her trip to New York. She began to read Dorothy Day's autobiography. When she finished, she read it right through again. Out of nowhere came the realization of what she wanted to do, what she wanted to be. In a stuffy little parlor at Holy Rosary she had her first talk with Father Justin. He was a Dominican; Holy Rosary was a Dominican parish. She tried to tell the priest what was on her mind.

He was in his sixties, she supposed, scruffy, despite the white habit with its clicking brown beads, hair sprouting from his ears, a prominent nose on which halfway down his glasses sat.

"Perhaps you have a vocation," he said, after she had babbled for twenty minutes.

"Not to be a nun!"

He laughed at her horror. "There are nuns and nuns, you know."

"Father, do you know about Dorothy Day?"

"Ah."

At first he treated it as simply a romantic impulse. He assigned spiritual readings. She began to go to Mass every day. She read the Little Hours from a book he gave her. *Shorter Christian Prayer.* "I have another edition for taller people," he said when he handed it to her.

She liked him. He was matter-of-fact.

What she wanted was to become holy, he told her. He gave her more books to read. "Do you say the rosary, Beth?"

She began to say the rosary every day. Working at Anderson's became more and more difficult. She talked with her parents, at the kitchen table in their house out by Minnehaha Falls. Her mother just listened, wide-eyed. Her father said, "You're nuts."

"Maybe it won't work out, Dad."

He looked out the window to where squirrels scampered on the lawns. "How much are we talking about?"

On the street floor of the building where she had her studio was an empty store. She would rent that. The kitchen was the big expense. The man who installed it had been recommended by Father Justin.

"What do you have in mind, a restaurant?"

"More like a soup kitchen."

"I can cook."

His name was Marvin, and he was her first volunteer. She scrounged around for furniture; Marvin put up shelves, and Beth filled them with books she got at Goodwill and St. Vincent de Paul. While the place was being prepared, men would shuffle by, slowing, stopping, looking in. Beth went out and told them when the grand opening would be. She designed the legend she put in the window. OUR LADY OF THE ROAD.

That's all it took. Father Justin came and blessed the place while the gentlemen of the road hung back. The aroma from the kitchen overcame any reluctance they might have felt at seeing a Dominican in full habit with a stole around his neck sprinkling holy water around.

So it had begun. Nearly twenty years ago. Father Justin had died, but one or another Dominican from Holy Rosary acted as chaplain of the center and as her spiritual director. People brought food and clothes, books. There were volunteers, most of them temporary, but some more or less permanent.

Like Timothy, who showed up one day like Lazarus.

4   WHENEVER JAY'S FATHER CALLED, HE seemed to be in a different place, Manhattan, somewhere in Connecticut—"a friend's place"—Florida, on campus. This time he was staying in the Inn at St. Mary's.

"Are you free for dinner, Jay?"

"Just tell me when and where."

"Bring Amanda, if you'd like."

"If she's free."

Of course his father had liked Amanda—how could he not—but things had not been going well with them since Jay had played his pranks on Roger Knight.

"Anaximenes," he had explained, showing her the poem.

"That's silly."

He looked at her. She looked away. "You're right," he said.

"What was the point?"

"I wanted to see how good a detective he is."

"Detective!"

"I thought of hiring him."

She lowered her head and glared at him.

"Amanda, I'm worried about my father."

He realized he really was worried about his father, but why? Belatedly it occurred to him that all the bad economic news must have affected his father's business and made enemies of people like

Larry Briggs. For so long he had been a wizard for his clients, but he had refused to take on the money Jay's mother had left him.

"Leave it where it is. Tax-free bonds are safe as houses." He stopped. "Not a good simile anymore. Phelps thinks I'm a riverboat gambler. That's okay. I only take on investors who can afford to lose as well as gain. You won't make much, Jay, but then you won't lose anything either. With me it could be a roller coaster."

Phelps, a lawyer, was in his seventies and spent most of his time now settling the estates of clients and looking after people like Jay who had inherited a claim on his time. Jay's maternal grandfather had been a client of Phelps's, and his mother had stayed with him. It was Phelps who had explained to Jay what his mother had left.

"Where did she get that kind of money?"

"From her father. I managed it for her." Phelps paused. "You might want your father to look after it now."

His father had refused. Phelps took this news phlegmatically. "Your only risk will be my age."

So the money had stayed with Phelps, in Philadelphia. At Phelps's suggestion Jay had just left it alone. When he met his father for dinner, he brought along his most recent statement from Phelps.

"Where's Amanda?"

"I wanted you all to myself."

His father punched his arm. Jay felt a surge of emotion and, as he had on other occasions, promised himself to be a better son. It occurred to him that his father was all alone, busy, lots of friends, certainly, and clients, but alone. They ordered drinks, and Jay handed his father the report from Phelps.

He nodded as he read it. "In the present market these gains look pretty good."

"How are you doing, Dad?"

"What do you mean?"

"How would I be doing if you were handling this money?"

"Not as well. At least during the past quarter."

"Would you want to take over?"

"No!" His father seemed embarrassed by the quickness with which he had refused. "Stay with Phelps, Jay. These are rocky times."

It was indirect, but Jay could see that things were not going well with his father. All the excited television chatter about the economy no longer seemed reports from elsewhere.

"How many clients like Briggs do you have?"

His father smiled, or tried to. "Briggs is Briggs. I'm no longer representing him."

"Dad, anytime you need my money, just say so."

His father looked at him in silence, then put a hand on Jay's. "It hasn't come to that."

Then he told Jay about putting the place on Longboat on the market and selling the boat. It all sounded worse than Jay had imagined. He told him, too, about disgruntled clients.

"Briggs."

"He was the worst. Some other clients didn't believe me when I'd warn them that what went up could come down. I don't think I believed that myself."

Jay remembered that Briggs had mentioned Mame Childers, but he hesitated to bring that up, not liking the uneasiness Briggs's mention of her name had given him. "But you're going to be all right?"

His father thought a bit, then leaned forward. "More than all right, Jay. A former classmate of mine who entered the Trappists left me a pile of money. Out of the blue. I learned that the last time I was here. At the time, I was sure I couldn't accept it. I've changed my mind."

"A Trappist classmate."

His father nodded.

"Did he tell you why?"

His father lifted his glass, then put it down. "I haven't asked him yet."

Dinner done, they had brandy, and his father told him about the friends he had made at Notre Dame. Pelligrino the Trappist; Casey the hack novelist; Beth Hanrahan, who ran a homeless center in Minneapolis; Mame Sayers, now Childers.

"Briggs mentioned her."

"She's a client," his father said quietly, not looking at Jay. He went on. "We were all idealists. Except for Mame. Do you know that, after your mother died, I thought of cashing in and living the simple life? Not the Trappists, not a homeless center, but out of the rat race. I wanted to recover the outlook I'd had as a student. You're living the most important years of your life now, Jay. I know you don't realize that, no one does at the time, but later . . ."

"What would the simple life have been?"

A wry smile. "It wouldn't be on Longboat Key."

"How about Siesta Key?"

"My classmate Casey lives there. There was another member of our group, Timothy Quinn, who disappeared."

"Come on."

"There's no other way to put it. None of us had any inkling it was coming, but one day he was gone."

"Where?"

"They dredged the lakes. And the river."

"Suicide?"

"We were all nuts about the same girl."

"Mame?"

His father laughed. "No, Beth. Mame was Casey's girl."

"They never found him?"

A slow meditative shaking of the head.

"What effort did they make?"

"I don't know the details. How do you go about locating a missing person? It was an awful thing to have happened. It broke up the old gang, I can tell you that. We all felt guilty somehow, like we should've known."

Jay sat forward. "They should have hired someone like Roger Knight and his brother. Private detectives."

"I don't think the university did anything like that."

"So it's still an unsolved mystery."

"Jay, he must be dead."

"But you don't know. Even finding that out would be something, wouldn't it? I think we should hire the Knight brothers and clear it up once and for all."

"But Knight is a professor now."

"His brother isn't."

5   PHILIP KNIGHT WAS WAKENED FROM
an afternoon nap by the doorbell.

It was Jay Williams. "Your brother introduced us."

"He's in class."

"I know. Can we talk?"

In his more active years, the criteria for a possible client were, first, money, and, second, something other than a routine task. Jay Williams was worried about his father. Phil doubted that the kid had money, and he was pretty vague about what worried him.

"You know my father is a financial adviser. I think he's taken a real hit."

"Is he despondent?"

The young man thought for a moment before shaking his head. "I wouldn't say that. Ever since my mother died he's led a whirlwind life, work, work, work, doing very well, and now this."

"How long ago did your mother die?"

"Three years."

"He hasn't remarried?"

"No! He'd never do that."

If he ever did, he clearly couldn't expect any understanding from his son. Phil had met Dave Williams right here in the apartment, when Father Carmody brought him. Midforties, maybe a little more.

"He is lonely," Jay conceded.

"What do you suspect?"

"Suspect? I don't suspect anything. I'm worried about him, that's all."

Phil let it go. There was no way in which he would take on such an assignment even though Jay mentioned that he had money of his own. Phil had always avoided divorce cases, and he wondered if the son's real worry wasn't that his still fairly young father might marry again. Say that was his plan; say Phil discovered this and reported to Jay. To what end? If Dave Williams decided on a second act for his life, his son would have to accept it. No doubt he would. Eventually.

"He keeps coming out here," Jay said. "I don't think he'd been on campus since my freshman year. Suddenly, he's a big benefactor, the generous alumnus, and here quite often."

When Phil's parents had died in an automobile accident, Roger was still a little kid, but Phil was older, and he always thought the loss hit him harder than it did Roger. The loss had propelled Phil into becoming his younger brother's guardian and provider. All along he had imagined himself filling in for their father. He graded himself by reference to what he imagined his father would have done, never in his own mind quite measuring up. Now that Roger was settled at Notre Dame, Phil had kept the agency but accepted almost no clients. If he had any hesitation about Jay Williams's confused request it was because he could imagine himself being that concerned about his own father.

"Will you do it?" Jay asked.

Phil looked away, moved by the expression on the young man's face. It was only the mention of Larry Briggs's visit that swayed him.

"Not officially. I don't want you as a client. I'll see if there is anything you need worry about."

He took Amtrak to New York, sleeping all the way, and spent a couple of days in Manhattan. He found it almost exhilarating to be back at work. The woman's name was Mame Childers, a divorcée. She and Dave had graduated the same year, she from St. Mary's, he from Notre Dame. She was a client of Dave's, but that didn't begin to describe the relationship. Phil heard about the place in Connecticut, rented a car, and went up there to take a look. A man emerged from the front door when Phil turned into the driveway. Phil got out of the car and waited for the man to come to him.

"Is this the Childers place?"

"It's not for sale." He was a big man, tall, massive chest, long arms, big feet. Very big feet. "I'm Wilfrid Childers."

They shook hands, and Phil looked around in unfeigned admiration. "It's hard to believe New York is so close."

"That's the point."

Had Wilfrid got the Connecticut place in the divorce settlement?

"You a New Yorker?" Childers asked.

"Not anymore."

"My plan was to retire here."

"Was?"

"My wife divorced me. We may remarry."

"Then your retirement plan may be revived."

Childers showed him around, the grounds, the woods with the little creek running through, the house and the little cottage. "I built this for my wife."

Phil also called on Larry Briggs, telling him that he lived in South Bend.

"I attended Notre Dame." Briggs looked as if Phil might deny this. He peered at him. "You on the faculty?"

"My brother is. Roger Knight."

"I get out there from time to time."

"Jay Williams mentioned that."

Briggs became flustered. "I was looking for his father. He lost a fortune for me."

"The son thinks you're stalking his father."

"Let him worry. The father."

Knowing more than he wanted to know about Dave Williams and the Childerses, and agreeing with Jay that Briggs was a nut, maybe even a dangerous nut, he returned to South Bend.

"Roger said you've been to New York," Jay said.

"That's right. On business."

"Mine?"

Phil had almost rehearsed what he would say to Jay Williams. "You have absolutely nothing to worry about."

"Did you see Larry Briggs?"

"Who is Larry Briggs?" But he laughed when he said it.

Phil was glad to get away to Minneapolis with Roger.

6   FATHER CARMODY HAD PLEADED HIS
erratic schedule, still active, likely to be
called hither and yon at any time, to exempt himself from the community concelebrated Mass at Holy Cross House. Gerry Maday, in his early sixties, superior of the place, had agreed but in a way that indicated he understood. It was Gerry's job, among others, to police the community Mass and make sure that no irregularities crept in, but given the average age and debility of residents that was a delicate task. The only time Father Carmody had taken part, pulling an alb over his head and draping one of the colorful stoles around his shoulders, he had sat next to an old priest, Johnson, whose chin was on his chest and who made blubbering sounds throughout. At the consecration, he had lifted his hand at the right moment but was deftly prevented from advancing to the altar for communion. Gerry eased him back into his chair and, chin still on his chest, the old fellow seemed to doze off. Some of the others didn't look to be in much better shape than Johnson.

"Old age is a shipwreck," Gerry said, nodding when Carmody went to him. So he understood Carmody's reason for asking to be held excused.

Of course, Gerry spoke as an observer. What a job he had. Did he see himself drifting from superior to inmate of the place? It was a somber thought that all of them, through all the years, no matter the work they were engaged in, had been on a glide path toward Holy Cross House.

At the crack of dawn, as that was computed in the house, Carmody had the chapel to himself and said his private Mass. That was the main job of the priest, saying Mass, and the office, too, of course. Those twenty-two minutes each morning connected Carmody's life with that long-ago day when he had lain prostrate in the sanctuary of Sacred Heart and been ordained a priest according to the order of Melchisedech. He could still vividly recall the sense of spiritual exaltation he had felt when his bound hands had been clasped in the bishop's, when the ordaining hands had been clamped firmly on his head, making him a priest. The ordinands concelebrated that Mass with the bishop, but that had been a once in a lifetime thing in those days. From then on, it was each man for himself, alone at the altar, with or without a congregation. For years, as president, Ted Hesburgh had said his daily Mass in a little closet of a chapel off the nave of the lower church, often at midday since he was always such a night owl, in his office until all hours, when students were not discouraged from dropping by. Ted had been the heart and soul of the place. For all the traveling he had done, he always seemed to be on campus.

After the Council, private Masses were frowned upon. Carmody had never understood the theology of the disapproval, if there was any. Half the nonsense that went on in those days was just made up. Change, that was the thing. Don't do anything the way it had always been done. Father Carmody had been young then, but you don't have to be old to hate arbitrary changes.

There were always several old priests at breakfast when he went in for his, early birds wanting first shot at the papers, a television set bringing in one of those mindless morning shows, the disasters of the day chirped merrily. My God, what a grump he had become. Even so, it was heaven to get back to his room, settle in his favorite chair, look out over the lake at the golden dome, and light his first cigarette of the day. His visitor was coming in on a morning flight, and he had arranged to have lunch with her at the Morris Inn. Lots of time. Mame Childers, née Sayers, St. Mary's '89. He couldn't remember her, but why should he? He would see Emil Chadwick before that.

Chadwick's house in Holy Cross Village, across the road, always made Carmody envious. Chock-full of books, a wonderful cluttered study, great views in two directions, full of the aroma of pipe tobacco. Chadwick was wearing slippers, baggy trousers, and a baggier sweater when he opened the door to Father Carmody. Chadwick stayed in the open doorway after he had let Carmody in. He had a pistol in his hand.

"Goddam Canada geese," he muttered. Half a dozen of these clumsy birds were progressing across Chadwick's lawn. He lifted his hand. Pfft. "Missed. Not that it matters. That is the most arrogant bird I have ever seen."

Chadwick closed the door.

"They're all over campus, too. What kind of gun is that?"

"A BB gun."

They went down the hall to Chadwick's sitting room. There were piles of books ten high on a round table in front of the couch. The plants seemed to be wilting. Pictures of Chadwick's wife and kids all over the place. One of the Trappist son.

"How is Brother Chrysologus?"

"He's a priest, you know, but they stick with Brother."

"What do they do with the old ones there?"

"There are men in their nineties who are always in their place in choir. They go until they drop."

Chadwick offered him coffee, but Carmody begged off. Chadwick's coffee was notoriously strong. There was a mug on one of the stacks of books, and Chadwick took it before settling into his chair.

"Roger wants to see Brother Joachim?"

Chadwick nodded. "I'm not sure why. The two of us may go to Gethsemani together. He asked me what I remembered of Timothy Quinn, the kid who disappeared."

"What did you tell him?"

"That Quinn actually read *Moby-Dick* all the way through."

There was no reason Chadwick shouldn't know about the packet that had arrived in the archives.

"Joachim claims Timothy Quinn was murdered."

Chadwick laughed, then stopped. "Seriously?"

"He wrote a story. Do you remember the group he was part of?"

"Vaguely."

"Mame Sayers?"

Chadwick thought for a minute. "A St. Mary's girl?"

"That's right."

"I could look it up. I think she took a course of mine."

"She was part of that group."

"Was she?"

"That's what she tells me."

"Roger Knight has asked me to take his seminar this afternoon."

"Is he ill?"

"Off on a trip. To Minneapolis. He wants to meet Beth Hanrahan."

On his way to the Morris Inn, driving by the nine holes of Burke Golf Course and the new residence whose name he could never remember, Father Carmody brooded. All this stirring up of the past boded no good.

7   THE PHOTOGRAPHS OF BETH HANRA-
han that Greg Walsh dug out of the archives
were not the usual sort that featured a large smile for the camera.
Her mouth dimpled at the corners as she looked with wide eyes into
the lens. Serene was the word that came to mind. A femme fatale?
Roger, a confirmed celibate, was no judge, and Greg was of little
help in that regard. A story dating from several years after her graduation told of the homeless center she had founded.

"How far is Minneapolis, Phil?"

"Five hundred miles or so."

"I'd like to go up there."

They checked into a motel on the outskirts of Minneapolis, on
I-494, separate units, and Roger told Phil to rest, he needn't come
to Our Lady of the Road.

"How would you get there?" Phil asked him.

"Cab?"

"Ha."

Well, he had wanted to give Phil the choice. "I'm going to take a
little nap."

"Good idea. Half an hour?"

"At most."

Lying on his back on the king-sized bed, arms behind his head, Roger stared unseeingly at the ceiling and thought about recent events. First there had been the arrival at the archives of the strange package from Brother Joachim, stirring up memories of long-ago events when Timothy Quinn had mysteriously disappeared from campus. The assumption had been that he was dead, a suicide, which God forbid, but dead in any case. Then came Brother Joachim's story claiming that his classmate had been killed and buried, saying where the body could be found. However, what was found under the boulder he had indicated was a decaying wooden box containing a hatchet and human remains, perhaps of a baby. Odd enough, that, but then there was the bequest to David Williams, who over the years had received an annual card from Gethsemani, the common message of which was, however indirect, repent. This suggested that Joachim in his letter had been describing a deed of David Williams's, not his own, but no deed of the kind he had described had been done, as Joachim would have known. So what had been the point of it all?

The bequest of money to David Williams, like those annual cards, was like an accusation. That had been Williams's first reaction, apparently, when he vowed not to accept it.

Three boys, the trinity as they were irreverently called, and the girl they had all unsuccessfully pursued, Beth Hanrahan. What she had done with her life made her interesting enough to visit even if it didn't cast any light on those confusing past events.

Roger had not managed to fall asleep before the phone rang and Phil suggested that they get going.

———

Beth threw up her hands in disbelief when Roger waddled across the room. He was quite a contrast to the lean and hungry men who lounged around the center.

"Dave said you were big, but . . ." She lowered her hands as if to display Roger to her beneficiaries, but her smile was welcoming, not mocking.

"Dave?"

"Williams. He called. After all these years. He thought I should be forewarned."

How to describe Beth Hanrahan? How had Homer described Helen? Launching a thousand ships was hardly comparable to a coed's having won the affection of three rivals, but even now, in her forties, there was that in Beth that told even an old celibate like Roger that here was an extraordinary person. Her thick, curly hair was white rather than gray; her hazel eyes were large and her mouth wide, the whole face the mirror of her soul, and it was the soul that came through. The dress she wore was shapeless, what their aunt Lucerne would have called a wash dress. Roger introduced Philip.

"Ah, the private detective."

Roger was looking around, fascinated. From the outside, it was simply a storefront with OUR LADY OF THE ROAD lettered on it, and beneath it WELCOME. In one corner of the large room was a rack on which old clothes hung, with beneath it a box of shoes. The furniture would have been used when she acquired it, and it had borne the weight of who knew how many wandering souls that had found their way here for a meal and some respite from their loneliness and defeat. On every face that stared at Roger he could read a different story of a life gone wrong, a will weakened to passivity.

Beth showed them around, glowingly proud of a center that for most would have seemed a desolate place, some level of ante-purgatory from which release was distant. The kitchen, with its massive stove on which a kettle simmered, giving off the aroma of stew, was in the charge of a tall, bearded fellow in a Cubs hat who kept backing away as if seeking invisibility.

Finally they settled in what she called her office, a box of a room with a dusty window, a table on which Roger noticed a little red book from which a golden ribbon peeked. There were chairs, but looking at them and then at Roger, Beth laughed. She went to the door. "Q, bring in one of the large chairs, would you?"

A minute later the man in the Cubs hat pushed in a more or less adequate chair, and Roger settled into it. The Cubs hat closed the door of the office when he left.

"So," Beth said when they were all seated.

"You say David Williams called you?"

"Isn't that amazing? After nearly twenty years. To think he once professed to be undyingly in love with me."

"I suppose he told you about the things Brother Joachim sent to the Notre Dame archives."

"He said he would leave that to you. At least Pat, Brother Joachim, sends me a Christmas card each year." She sighed. "Sometimes I'm tempted to escape to a convent."

"Escape?"

"Elsewhere always seems easier, doesn't it?"

Phil picked up a magazine from the table, looked at it, put it back. Beth thought he must be wishing he had stayed at the motel. She said to him, "So what are you detecting?"

"Roger tells a better story than I do."

Roger told her then of Joachim's donation to the archives. "It was all about the disappearance of his classmate Timothy Quinn. He claimed to have killed him."

"That's absurd."

"Well, it's false. He wrote a story about it," Phil said.

"That's why I brought it along." Roger handed her the story, and she hunched in her chair as she read it. Then she read it again.

"Just a story," she said, giving it back to Roger.

"He described where he had buried the body, but all that was found there was a hatchet and what looked like human bones."

"Where did he say he buried the body?" Her manner had changed, and she leaned anxiously toward Roger as she asked.

"Do you remember the Log Chapel?"

"Oh my God."

"I've told you all that was found. Joachim also left David Williams a considerable amount of money."

"Where would a monk get money?"

"He had made the bequest before entering Gethsemani. He had inherited it from an uncle."

"And he gave it to David Williams?"

"That surprises you?"

She thought for a moment. "I don't know why it should, but it does."

"Perhaps because he was a rival."

"Oh, he was never that."

"No."

"Sometimes I think that the only one of the three I really loved was David. Of course, that's hindsight. Water long since over the dam."

"Where on earth do you think Quinn went when he disappeared?"

The chair she sat in was a swivel chair, relic of some long-ago office. She turned in it slowly as if in search of true north. Then she rose. "Excuse me for a moment."

When they were alone, Phil said, "Well, it was a nice drive anyway."

"What do you think of her?"

"Is she a nun?"

"Not quite."

The door opened and Beth came back, alone, a frown on her face. "He's gone."

"Who?"

"Q. Timothy. Timothy Quinn."

8 AFTER BETH HANRAHAN'S AMAZING statement that Timothy Quinn was alive and well and working with her at Our Lady of the Road, Phil rushed off to try to locate the man who had a habit of disappearing.

Beth dismissed any suggestion that there was something amiss in her keeping Timothy Quinn's secret. "Who could be hurt by his absence? He has no relatives to speak of. Besides, it was all so long ago."

"Unfortunately, interest in the matter has been stirred up by Brother Joachim's contribution to the Notre Dame archives."

She considered that. "What on earth did he expect to accomplish?"

"He seemed convinced that Timothy had come to a violent end."

"That's nonsense."

"Surely you didn't think at the time Quinn had just evaporated."

She was silent for a moment. "No. His disappearance had a devastating effect on all of us."

The conversation could have gone on, in circles, but Roger returned to the fascinating topic of Beth's refuge for the hungry and homeless. "Do you live here?"

"Oh, no. I kept the studio upstairs after I opened the center."

"Studio."

"I was an aspiring artist."

"Is that yours?"

On the wall was a picture in the form of a stained glass window featuring Dorothy Day. It was Beth's.

"So you haven't given it up?"

"I don't have much time for it now, but it is a blessed relief when things get hectic here."

"Could I see the studio?"

"You'll have to climb some steep stairs."

Roger heaved himself to his feet and threw back his shoulders, an alpine climber about to brave the Matterhorn. "No problem," he said. "No problem at all."

She was right about the stairs. There was a railing set rather insecurely in the wall on which it would have been unwise to rely. At the top of the stairs, Beth opened the door, and a breathless Roger walked in to face the man in a Cubs cap. Timothy Quinn. He looked accusingly at Beth. Had she advised him to take refuge in her studio?

"Q," she said, "you've done nothing wrong. Please relax."

Timothy Quinn looked like one of Beth's guests rather than a co-worker—spare and rangy, a tousled beard, wild hair escaping from the edges of his cap. He wore bib overalls and a flannel shirt. He had kicked off his cowboy boots and was in socks that exhibited his big toes to the world.

"Take those off, Q, and I'll darn them."

Obediently Timothy Quinn sat and began to pull off his woolen socks.

Roger had gone to the easel and was studying the half-finished portrait there. "David Williams?" he asked.

"His telephone call prompted that. I'm working from photographs, newspaper photographs. Go ahead and say it, it's not very good."

Quinn joined Roger at the easel and glared at the canvas. "That sonofabitch."

Not a propitious note on which to tell him of what Brother Joachim had sent to the Notre Dame archives. "He thought you had been killed by Dave Williams."

"He's the one who should have been killed. That's why I took off."

"You were afraid?"

"Afraid that I would kill him if I didn't."

"They found your hatchet, Q," Beth said.

"Where?"

Roger described digging beneath the boulder that Brother Joachim had said marked the remains of Timothy Quinn. Beth listened nervously.

"What is Pat up to, Beth?" Quinn asked.

"I think I know," Beth said.

Roger and Q waited, but she did not go on. "It's nothing important."

"Tell me," Roger urged.

"It's personal."

It was half an hour later that Phil came up the stairway to the studio. He looked at Quinn with disgust, the reaction of a man who had just returned from a wild goose chase. He asked Beth for the use of her phone and called the police, telling them to call off the search for Timothy Quinn.

Prompted by Beth, Timothy Quinn told the story of his long-ago disappearance. He had gone out to the toll road entrance booth and managed to get a ride to Chicago. From there he took the train to California. San Diego. The manual jobs he took paid better than he would have thought and all the beaches made it seem he was on vacation. After several years of that, he enlisted in the army and ended up getting shot at in Baghdad. Eventually, he received a serious wound and was flown off to a hospital ship. His enlistment ended while he was recovering, and he reenlisted. It seemed the line of least resistance. Finally, he ended up back in San Diego, with another chance to renew his life. Nurses had brought him back editions of the South Bend paper and he read about his disappearance and presumed death. After discharge, he drifted back to Indiana with the vague idea that he would tell someone what had happened. Back on campus, he found that the hidden life still had him in its grips.

"You went back to Notre Dame?"

"I got a job on the grounds crew at the golf course, mowing fairways, watering greens. After work, I would wander around the campus, remembering."

"How long were you there?"

"Just the one summer. It was all changed."

Then he came upon a write-up of the work Beth was doing in Minneapolis. His tone altered as he spoke of Beth and it was clear that his long-ago love had survived his wanderings.

"It was weeks before he told me who he was," Beth said. "I thought he was kidding, but all he had to do was recall those days and I knew he was who he said he was. So I let him stay."

Quinn's brown eyes rolled to her as a dog's might roll to its mistress. One of his feet began to thump upon the floor.

"He's not much help," she said cheerily, "but like the others, he has no place to go."

At the far end of the studio was a bed, the area marked off by a planter luxuriant with forty shades of green. A suspicious mind might have wondered how far the reunion of Beth and Quinn had taken them. Roger dismissed the thought as unworthy. Whatever Quinn's interpretation of her willingness to let him stay, it clearly differed from hers.

As was his habit, Roger was now wandering around inspecting whatever books were in the studio. *"The Woman Who Was Poor,"* he cried. "Léon Bloy."

"Is that how you pronounce it?"

Roger opened the book and read. "'There is only one tragedy, not to be a saint.'"

"Isn't that lovely?" Beth said.

Quinn looked despondent.

"You and Dave Williams ought to get together," Roger suggested.

"It's a little late for that." There was a wistful tone in her voice. Quinn got up and kicked one of his boots across the room.

"What now?" Phil said.

"We have accomplished our mission," Roger said. "Timothy, would you mind coming back to Notre Dame with us, to help clear things up?"

"Not on your life."

"I'll come with you and explain everything," Beth said suddenly. "Q can look after things while I'm gone."

9 A STIPULATION OF BETH HANRAH-
an's returning to Notre Dame was that abso-
lutely no fuss was to be made. She would explain what had happened,
remove any lingering sense of fault on the part of the university, and
then return to her work in Minneapolis. For all that, the trip was so
much a departure from what had become the even tenor of her ways
that she begged to be taken to the new shrine of Our Lady of Gua-
dalupe at La Crosse, Wisconsin, a stop that did not take them far
out of their way. They stayed overnight in La Crosse since Beth did
not want simply to pop in and out of the shrine but to attend Mass as
well.

Her second suggestion, an Orthodox church in Chicago where an
icon of Mary was said to weep, was more difficult. It took Phil hours
to find the place, relying on questioning several startled pastors at
whose rectories they stopped. When Phil pulled into a mall and
noticed there was a church on the opposite side of the street, he said
he would make one last effort.

A bearded priest listened to him with cocked head and narrowed
eyes. "You are joking, yes?"

"I am only telling you what I've heard. A weeping icon."

"But this is the place!"

Beth knelt for half an hour before the icon, kissed the priest's
hand, and whispered to Roger, "Give him something."

Roger handed the bearded priest a twenty-dollar bill. He was holding it up to the light as they left.

Chattering on the road, Beth had asked if Father Carmody was still alive.

"That's his story," Phil said.

"He must be ancient."

"Did you know him?"

"He was my spiritual adviser. What I'll do is just explain everything to him and go on back to the center."

"There is a direct flight to Minneapolis from South Bend."

She looked at Phil. "I'll go by bus. Did you ever hear the story of Dorothy Day coming to Notre Dame by bus when she received the Laetare Medal?"

"Have you ridden a bus lately?"

She ignored him. "I had forgotten about Gary," she said, as they slipped through the gritty town on the Indiana toll road. Even with the windows up the smell was unmistakable. An hour later, they left the toll road and stopped at the booth, with Beth's alma mater, St. Mary's College, looking like a picture.

"How I hated that place." Just an observation; there was no bitterness in her voice. "A women's college. I only went there because I was turned down by Notre Dame. I spent most of my time on the Notre Dame campus."

Soon they were coming down Notre Dame Avenue with the golden dome visible before them, Mary on its top, looking in their direction. Beth gave a little cry.

"This is the first time I've been here in I don't know how many years. I am so glad I've come."

The question now was where she was to stay. There was no extra bedroom in the Knights' apartment, which was their first stop. Beth got out the phone book while the brothers fidgeted. In a moment she was dialing the number of a South Bend homeless center with the catchy name of Our Lady of the Road. Whoever answered told her she wanted Baxter.

"Is he there?"

"Hold on."

Within minutes, she had been offered a room in the center's women's residence.

"Staying in motels could spoil me," she said to Roger.

Off she went with Phil, leaving it to Roger to set up an appointment with Father Carmody so she could tell him all about it. Phil had wanted to call Carmody after the discovery of Quinn in Minneapolis, but Roger urged the delay.

"Beth Hanrahan?" Father Carmody asked.

"She said you used to be her spiritual director."

"I don't give refunds."

Meanwhile, Roger put through a call to David Williams, thinking that he should know how things had developed. Brother Joachim? That could wait.

10 THERE IS A BLACK BOX INTO WHICH a priest places the sins he is told and the confidences he receives, not only in the confessional but in any conversation in which a person clearly regards what he or she is saying as between him or herself and God, the priest there merely as the viceroy of the latter. Now that penitents could choose to confess face-to-face, something that in the past had occurred only rarely and outside the confessional box, the confessor could not help but connect the sin and the sinner. Father Carmody continued to hear student confessions in Sacred Heart, and as often as not the penitent would come around the grille and sit facing him as he told the anguished tale. Carmody had opposed this, as he had most innovations, but had come grudgingly to think it had its points. It certainly did not make keeping the seal of the confessional any more difficult. For Carmody it had never been difficult at all. Spiritual direction was another matter. Face-to-face then, all right, but he would be damned if he would call confession reconciliation. It made sin seem a quarrel between equals.

From the very first time that the long-ago disappearance of Timothy Quinn had been raised by Brother Joachim's contribution to the Notre Dame archives and the names of the young men began being tossed about, the name of the girl, Beth Hanrahan, had put Father Carmody on the alert. He had known the young men, but he had been privy to the secrets of Beth Hanrahan's soul. Had he known her before she had come to him in his role as priest? Not well, if at all. Her nervousness, her expression, told him how seriously she regarded what she had come to tell.

"Father, I don't know how to begin."

"Is it a boy?" With penitents the age Beth was then, sexual faults were usually the burden borne.

"Yes!" She seemed to think he had made an uncanny guess.

In those days, Father Carmody had a suite of rooms on the ground floor of Sorin Hall from the windows of which he could look out at the entrance of Sacred Heart. It was a men's dorm, so it was something of a surprise when he found that it was a girl who had come to his door.

"Tell me about it," he said. "No details!"

"We made love."

Well, he hardly expected her to confess to fornication. Often boys claimed to have committed adultery though neither they nor their partner was married. It seemed pedantic to correct them.

"Have you confessed this?"

She seemed surprised. "That's what I'm doing."

He opened a drawer, took out a stole, and draped it purple side out over his shoulders. No need to ask her to say again what she considered already confessed.

"There must be no repetition."

She shook her head. "No."

"Will you see him again?"

Her hesitation was the answer to that.

"Tell him you have confessed. Tell him to do the same."

For her penance he told her to say five decades of the rosary. He gave her absolution while she was making an act of contrition, the familiar Latin words rolling off his tongue. *Ego te absolvo, in nomine Patris, et Filii, et Spiritus Sancti.*

"Thank you, Father."

She stood, and for a moment he thought she might ascend to the ceiling, so visible was her relief. He said nothing more while she left and closed the door behind her.

A week later, she was back, bearing the same burden. Then two weeks went by, and again she came to confess the same sin.

"This can't go on, you know. Of course, you might marry."

The thought seemed never to have occurred to her. Well, she was young, a student, maybe only a year or two older than Carmody's mother had been when she got married, but things had changed. If these impulses could be worked out in an appropriate way at the age when they were most difficult to resist, things would be better. As it was, temptation continued, and lapses. The main thing was not to let repetition bring on despair. God is merciful.

The next time she came she was pregnant.

As if released from being kept under decades of pressure, these memories came back to Father Carmody when Roger called to tell him that Beth Hanrahan wished to see him. "What brought her down?"

"That's what she wants to talk about."

"Did you have any luck in Minneapolis?"

"You'll be surprised."

"I hate surprises."

11   MIKE BAXTER, WHO RAN THE COUN-
terpart of Beth's Minneapolis center in South
Bend, offered to give Beth a lift to campus, but she availed herself
of public transportation and got off the bus at the library. Coming
onto campus with the Knight brothers didn't count. She wanted to
see it alone and let the sweet sad thoughts come. She headed for the
powerhouse, then took a path around the lake to Holy Cross House,
where she would meet Father Carmody.

"I will fit you into my crowded schedule," he had said on the
phone.

"Your voice hasn't changed."

"I was a mere boy when it did."

Coming up to the building from the lake, it became clear to her
that none of these doors was used as an entrance, so she went
around the building and found Father Carmody seated by the door,
smoking a cigarette. He looked up at her, the same gruff face, but
welcoming nonetheless. When he stood, he hesitated. Would he embrace her? But that had not been the practice when he was young,
and she had the comforting thought that the old priest was the same
person who had been young. She took his hand in both of hers.

He punched some number into a gadget beside the door, and it
slid open. They went past a nursing station and down a long hallway

to the end. His rooms overlooked the lake. They sat for a time in a comfortable silence, and then he said, "The last time we spoke you were pregnant."

"I lost the baby."

His brows lowered. "Lost it?"

"Stillborn. I wanted to come tell you that, but I didn't."

"God works in mysterious ways."

"It changed my life."

He nodded. "Tell me about your work in Minneapolis."

She did, downplaying the success of the center and her own role.

"How long has Timothy Quinn been working there?" He had pried this out of Phil.

She had to think. "Seven or eight years, off and on. He comes and goes."

"Did he ever consider what he had put others through by just disappearing like that?"

"That was my fault."

"How?"

"I told him I was pregnant." Her expression was a stricken one. "I had to tell someone; I just blurted it out."

"Was he the father? You don't have to answer that."

"No, he wasn't."

"Pelligrino?"

"No. Oh, no. Although he helped me bury the baby. I won't call her a fetus."

"Bury it?"

It was clear that Father Carmody had never wondered what happened when a woman miscarried. Did he think it was like changing your mind?

"Yes. We buried it close to the back wall of the Log Chapel. I had baptized it—her—and it seemed as close as I could get her to consecrated ground."

"The back wall of the Log Chapel."

"The west end."

"My God."

"Surely that wasn't wrong."

"No, of course not. Have you been told of the strange letter Brother Joachim wrote?"

"Leaving money to David Williams?"

"No, this was another letter. A confessional story."

"Yes, I've read it."

"Well?"

"It's fiction. For the most part."

"Pelligrino seemed to claim that Timothy Quinn had been killed and was buried near the chapel. The grave was marked by a boulder. When we dug there, we found a rotted box and a hatchet." He looked away. "And some bones."

"He did want to kill Timothy," she said, and he turned back to her.

"Why?"

She looked around the cluttered room, at the desk with books and papers piled on it, at the books on the floor beside his easy chair, one leaning against the stand that held his massive ashtray. How comfortable it seemed.

"He thought Timothy was the father."

She could see that the old priest was thinking of that long-ago trinity of friends, two of whom she had excluded.

"Because of Pat's threat to kill Tim, I couldn't tell him that it was David Williams."

"Did you tell David?"

"No."

"You told Quinn. Pelligrino knew. Yet you didn't tell the father."

"I told Pat in a moment of weakness. When I calmed down, I couldn't think of a way to tell Dave that wouldn't sound like a claim on him."

"You had a claim on him, as did the child."

"After I lost the baby . . ."

Father Carmody lit a cigarette. Smoke from the one he had just ground out still rose from his ashtray.

"Then why would Pelligrino, knowing the truth, write that incredible story?"

"Perhaps he thinks I haven't suffered enough," she said quietly.

Speaking of these things, she felt again the oddity of having been pursued by three friends, each of whom claimed to love her. What had happened with David had not, of course, been planned; it had surprised them both, and once done lowered her defenses. Although they had spoken of marriage, she had not told him when she became pregnant. Her condition seemed to turn her in upon herself, making her realize that this predicament was hers in a way that it could never be his. The odd thing was that she had told the other two of her condition, Timothy because he was there when she was in her first panic, Patrick after the miscarriage. She was overcome with sorrow and shame. Why had she chosen to tell Pat? Because he was the one she found when she went to their room, looking for David. She was carrying her burden wrapped in a towel. She had taken Patrick's arm and led him outside. He stared at her in disbelief when she told him what they were going to do.

"He dug the hole with a hatchet."

Even after all these years, she felt she could read Patrick's mind, as she could read Timothy's. Somehow it had occurred to him that the father of her dead baby was David Williams. First, though, he had accused Timothy. That was the night before he disappeared.

"He wanted revenge?"

"I can't believe that could be his motive."

"What, then?"

She sat in silence for a moment. She might have been inside Brother Joachim's mind. When she spoke it was in a low but steady voice.

"Maybe he thinks that what we did, burying the baby, was wrong." There were tears in her eyes. "I know that's what I think."

(12) AT THE OLD BASTARDS TABLE IN
Leahy's Lounge, the aged emeriti were happy
to have a topic they could get their dentures into.

"He didn't disappear," Potts protested. "He appeared somewhere else."

Armitage Shanks affected patience. "My dear fellow, you are giving the definition of 'disappear.' No longer appearing in one place. He is here. On campus. Pfft. He's elsewhere."

Horvath was remembering the moving memorial service that had been held for the presumably dead student Timothy Quinn. "Everyone wept."

"Now there can be tears of joy. He who was lost has been found."

"He wasn't lost," Potts grumbled.

The story had appeared in both the *Observer* and the alternative student paper, the *Irish Rover*, bumping wire service stories from the front page of the former and displacing the latter's Obama Watch, a feature headed by a picture, two columns wide, of a Mickey Mouse wristwatch. The source of the story was Jay Williams, son of one of the students involved in that long-ago event. Both papers wrote of it as if it were some impossibly ancient happening, but then it had occurred before many of them were born.

"There wasn't this much fuss when he went away."

Once more they toasted Timothy Quinn. Thus fortified, Shanks suggested that the administration had manufactured this issue to draw attention away from the awful buildings that were sprouting up on campus in the midst of economic troubles. He had brought a clipping telling the story of suspension of work on a new skyscraper in Manhattan.

"Harvard is cutting staff by twenty-five percent," Bingham said with relish. "Their obscene endowment has decreased by nearly that fraction."

"How are we doing?"

"*We?*" Three pairs of eyes regarded Potts.

"The university's endowment."

"*We* have nothing to do with that, Potts. Or perhaps you have been consulted about investments."

Potts said a vulgar word, and Shanks burst into song. "Where never is heard a cloacal word . . ."

Murph the bartender came and tapped him on the shoulder. "This is a respectable place."

"In what respect?"

"Anyone ready for another?"

Everyone was ready for another. It seemed the least they could do to celebrate the finding of whatshisname, Timothy Quinn. Shanks repeated that he had had the boy in class, and yes, he had kept all his grade books.

"For light reading?"

"I have spent whole evenings with them."

"Armitage, sometimes I think you live solely for pleasure," Bingham said.

It was the Notre Dame alumnus now a Trappist monk in Kentucky that captured the secularized imaginations of the current crop of students. The *Irish Rover* was sending a reporter to interview Brother Joachim in his cell.

"Isn't it *Irish Setter?*"

Potts said, as if continuing a thought, "Do you realize there isn't a men's room on this floor?"

"Scandalous." Relief was always a stairway away. The design of the Morris Inn could not be blamed on the current administration, though, so the topic drifted away. So did Potts, pursuing his thoughts.

13 ----------➤ "WHY DON'T YOU COME HERE?" MAME
Childers said when David Williams called to
say he wanted to see her.

"This is business. Come to my office."

She spent the morning getting dolled up for the appointment. Peaches had called from Florida to say that the asking price for David's place on Longboat Key had dropped to the level where she had said her interest would kick in.

"Give me twenty-four hours."

"If that doesn't go through, there are loads of other properties."

"That's the only one I'm interested in."

It would be her trump card, telling David that he wouldn't be losing the condo on Longboat Key. In recent days, she had been asking around, trying to find out just how badly David Williams LLC had been hit by the economic downturn.

"Hard," Pincus said.

"Hard as in how much?"

"Like many others, he is going to have to wait a long time for the market to bring him back."

"Are you among them?"

Pincus dropped his chin. "Your statement should give you the answer to that."

"How do you do it?"

"Bonds, and we are going into banks while bank stock is down." He sat back, a picture of self-approval. "A recession that ruins some is the making of others."

The money she had put with David had dropped 40 percent, a loss that was tolerable because of all the money she had with Pincus.

"What about Wilfrid?"

Pincus frowned. "Like you, he has money invested elsewhere as well."

Elsewhere and apparently unwisely. Recently they had had dinner at a once favorite restaurant of theirs and been welcomed as if nothing had changed. Well, theirs was a civilized Manhattan divorce.

"Like old times," Wilfred said, leaning toward her across the table. He lifted his glass. "To us."

What was this? She was right to be wary. He looked into her eyes, the look of a lover, and asked what in hell they had gained by splitting up. "You're single, I'm single. All it did was double our costs. I miss the place in Connecticut."

"Will, you're welcome to use it anytime. Just give me advance warning."

"Warning?"

"A figure of speech."

"David Williams?"

"You've been spying."

"People notice. How serious is it?"

"Well, aren't you nosy. We're not engaged, if that's what you're after."

"Not engaged," he repeated. "I never liked that sonofabitch."

"Oh, come on."

"There are Catholics and Catholics. Your kind I can understand."

"I'm not much of a one."

"You're enough for me." His hand came across the table and rested on hers. "Tell me you miss me."

"Of course I miss you."

"How much has he lost for you?"

"Lots."

He grew serious. "I've been hit hard myself."

Aha. "Pincus will bring us through."

"I wish I had put everything with him."

She looked at the somber man who had been her husband, a man she once had loved. The thought that she and Will could come together again was not unpleasant. Call it a fallback position. Even so, she was determined not to let David Williams get away.

David's offices in the Chrysler Building gave no sense that he had fallen on hard times. The receptionist was bright and chipper, with a skirt scarcely reaching her knees. His administrative assistant, Della Portiere, was brisk and efficient in her pin-striped suit, whose skirt came almost to midcalf. She ushered Mame into David's office. He was on the phone; he fluttered his hand apologetically, indicating that she should sit. She sat.

"Thanks, Father. Thanks for letting me know."

He hung up and swung toward her, all business.

"Father?"

"Father Carmody. You won't believe this. Timothy Quinn has turned up alive."

"I *don't* believe it."

"Alive and well and working with Beth Hanrahan in Minneapolis."

The topic got them off on a comfortable footing, bringing back those wonderful years in South Bend. David seemed as relieved as she was to have this vast diverting topic to begin her appointment. They recalled the first days after Timothy's disappearance, the sense of guilt that had gripped Patrick Pelligrino and David. Beth, too, of course.

"It was never the same afterward. Mame, sometimes I think that I am the only one who came out of it to live a halfway normal life. Patrick down there in Kentucky as Brother Joachim; Beth running a soup kitchen in Minneapolis and taking in Tim Quinn when he surfaced."

"Where on earth was he?"

"Much of the time in the army, as an enlisted man. All in all, he apparently put in twelve years."

"What a shock it must have been for Beth when he walked in the door."

"Father Carmody says she didn't recognize him at first. He volunteered, she put him to work, and only gradually did she realize who he was."

"You have to tell Casey and Peaches."

He frowned. "I sold my boat."

"So I heard. Peaches showed me around the place on Longboat."

"I wish she'd sell it." He shook his head. "No I don't. How I'll miss that place."

"You don't have to."

"What do you mean?"

"I may put in a bid on it."

His reaction was not what she had hoped. He glared at her. "Why in hell would you do that?"

"Because I don't want you to lose it."

"Mame, even if you bought it—"

"Don't say it, Dave."

"The fact is, I may take it off the market. I've decided to accept the money Pat Pelligrino gave me. That's the point of our meeting today. Mame, I want to make up what you've lost with me. I'll buy you out entirely, if you want."

"I don't want! I want to be with you."

"We've been through that."

"Dave, I've talked again with my monsignor. He will write a letter stating his opinion. He is miffed to have his expertise questioned. Dave, there is no obstacle!"

He looked at her in silence. Obviously, this was not the conversation he had planned to have. "Mame, I can never marry again. It's not just a legal matter with me. My son . . ."

Patience, patience. "I understand. All right, we won't get married." She had surprised him. "We will just go back to the way we were."

She watched the thought settle in. Had it been the fear of marriage that had spoiled everything? Well, after all, he was a man. Tender memories seemed to come to him; she could read them on his face. For the first time since she had sat across his desk, he relaxed.

"I have missed you."

"Have you now?"

When she rose to go, they had agreed to meet for drinks at five.

"Mame, I meant it about your money."

"What kind of woman do you take me for?"

He came around his desk and took her in his arms before escorting her past Della Portiere.

It was several hours after Mame left his office that Della told him that a Mr. Childers wished to see him.

"Is he on the phone?"

"He's here."

"Show him in."

This was a surprise. Dave had met Mame's husband once or twice but knew him mainly through the filter of Mame's description of their marriage. He rose to meet his visitor. Childers strode across the room, full of the pride of life, and thrust a hand at David.

"Wilfrid Childers. We've met. Forgive this impromptu call, but I was in the building . . ."

"Not at all. Delighted to see you. Would you like coffee?"

"Yes, I would."

Dave nodded to Della, and Childers sat and looked around. "Nice office."

"If I can keep it."

Childers looked at him, rubbed his face with his hand, shook his head. "It's been bad for a lot of people. How's the market today?"

"Pretty much like yesterday."

Della brought the coffee; they sipped. Childers put down his cup. "I didn't come to discuss the market, Williams. There's something you should know about Mame and me. As you know, we're divorced. It seemed right at the time. Now second thoughts occur." He said all this in a rush, as if he had rehearsed it.

Dave settled back, unable completely to erase the image of Mame seated in that same chair just hours before. There seemed no need to respond to what Childers had said.

"You can understand why I'm telling you this."

"I think I'd like an explanation."

"I know you've been seeing a bit of Mame. Why not? She's a free woman, and a damned attractive one." He paused. "You've been up in Connecticut?"

"Wonderful place."

"People just drive in and want to buy it. Sometimes I think I miss it more than I miss Mame." He frowned. "That's a joke. A bad joke." A pensive look came over his ruddy face. "I know Mame has lost money. What would you say to my opening an account with you?"

"Surely you have a financial adviser?"

"Advisers. I'm not suggesting I would go exclusively with you. How much did Mame lose?"

"I can hardly tell you that."

Childers thought about it. "Of course not. My point is that if a client loses, you lose. Right?"

"Sometimes I lose the client."

"Would you like to gain one?"

The offer was such an obvious ploy that Dave figured he was meant not only to see that but, seeing it, to leave it uncommented on. Childers bursts into his office, informs him that he is having second thoughts about being divorced from Mame, then offers to open an account with a man who had lost a considerable sum of his former wife's money. Obvious as it was, it was less crude than simply offering him money to leave Mame alone.

"There's no need to open an account with me, Wilfrid."

"How so?"

"It's because of me and Mame, isn't it?"

"Are you going to marry her?"

Dave was silent for a moment. "We've talked about it, yes."

"And?"

"I think I've said enough. I can imagine how difficult it is for you to ask these questions. You have the answer you came for."

Childers considered that. Let him put two and two together for himself. Apparently he did. He rose. "I know what she's like. Don't marry her."

Childers's expression was pathetic. Is it only when we've lost something that we want it? He thought of Bridget. Compared to his own attitude toward Mame, Childers's seemed almost noble.

"I don't know what I'd do if she married again."

What was he to say to that?

"Don't think that I'm threatening you."

"Because you are?"

"Maybe."

"You problem is with Mame, not me."

"And you're her problem." He stood. "I feel like a fool, but I'm glad I came."

"So am I."

They actually shook hands again. May the best man win? Take your wife, please. On the way to the door, Childers turned. "I meant that about opening an account with you."

Dave lifted his hands, displaying his palms, and then Childers was gone.

The midtown bar was packed with the late afternoon crowd, stags at eve mainly, but one or two women.

Mame was waiting for him inside the door. "This place is a zoo, Dave. We'll never get a table."

"Let's go somewhere else."

"I know a place."

Outside she hailed a cab, and when they got in she gave her own address. Her knees were pressed against his. He pressed back.

Wilfrid's visit to his office seemed to have conferred invulnerability on him. No need to invoke Father Carmody's imaginary veto now. He could always play the Wilfrid card. Going to her place no longer seemed compromising. He had tired of his role as the pursued lover, and Wilfrid had provided him with a defense..

When they emerged from the elevator into her front hall, she cried, "Oh, this is so much better."

He took her coat. She lifted her face and, why not, he gave her a passionate kiss. She stepped back, eyes widened. "You make the drinks. I'll be right back."

He was sipping his drink when she floated into the living room barefoot, wearing a silken robe that rose and fell with her movements.

"Comfortable?" he asked, handing her a glass.

"I'm always comfortable with you."

She sat next to him, and again her knees pressed against his. She lifted her face. Why not? He took her in his arms and was filled with a fierce ardor. His role now seemed that of the macho male who takes his pleasure where he finds it, flitting from flower to flower. Not that this would lead to anything. He would lose his advantage if they went down the hall. Ten minutes later, he was still telling himself that as they went down the hall to her bedroom.

Afterward she was in a playful mood, and he held her tightly, almost in self-defense. Then like an idiot he just blurted it out. "Wilfrid came to my office this afternoon."

She sprang free and, kneeling on the bed, glared down at him. "That is a very bad joke."

"I wish it were. He told me he regrets the divorce."

He had never seen her throw a real tantrum before. Her anger was directed against Wilfrid, at least at first, but he came in for his share of vituperation. Why hadn't he told her that immediately? Why hadn't he . . . She didn't know what he should have done, only that he should have done it. Finally she subsided and tried to snuggle, whimpering in his arms.

"He's just trying to make trouble."

"He seemed quite in earnest."

"He's always in earnest."

"He offered to open an account with me."

"Surely you didn't agree."

"I never divulge professional confidences."

After a long minute, she smiled. "You already have."

If once, why not twice? He could hate himself afterward twice as much. Even during, there was the nagging thought that he would have to go to confession. This wasn't wrong because he had to confess it, humbling as that was. He had to confess because it was wrong. No need to go into that with Mame. Think of it as a professional secret.

14 IT WAS GREG WALSH WHO BECAME
interested in the diary that had been in-
cluded in the stuff Brother Joachim had sent to the archives.

"I had forgotten that," Roger said. "Weren't most of the pages
empty?"

"Yes." Greg pushed the diary across the table to Roger. They
were seated at a table in the archives. Greg had taken on some of
the characteristics of the treasures he spent the day with, musty,
timeless, at least of another time.

Roger read the entry Greg indicated. *"Infans sepelitur."* He
looked at Greg. "We found a hatchet, and perhaps the remains of a
baby."

"Maybe he named the hatchet. Like Excalibur."

Roger looked at the previous page in the diary. "'DW! Oh, God,
God.'"

"What do you make of it?"

"He seems to have known Latin."

Roger shut the diary and laid his enormous hand on its padded
cover, as if the diary would communicate with him. "Let me take
this, Greg. I'll sign out for it."

"When I stop trusting you I'll enter the monastery myself."

Having gone down in the elevator, through the stile, and into the
lobby of the Hesburgh Library, Roger realized that he was cradling

the diary. *Infans sepelitur.* The baby is buried. Strange—but then all those long-ago events were strange when one tried to piece them together after a lapse of two decades. Phil had lost patience with the whole thing and growled when Roger brought home the diary. The reappearance of Timothy Quinn in Beth Hanrahan's center still rankled. He felt that he had been toyed with. He reminded Roger of the silly damned poem he had received.

"That was from a current student."

"The son of Dave Williams." He said it as if saying QED. "It runs in the family."

"The diary is Pelligrino's."

"The whole bunch of them were living in a dream world."

Roger took the diary into his study and got settled in the specially built chair that enabled him to propel himself about the room, from desk to computer to bookshelves and back. A code? No. He was being influenced by Phil's reminder of the poem Jay Williams had slipped under his door to test his investigative powers. The entry could not refer to the hatchet they had found after following Brother Joachim's instructions as Greg had thought. Recalling that scene, with Phil and Jimmy Stewart stepping back from the hole so that he and Father Carmody could see what they had unearthed, Roger remembered the sense of letdown. They had dreaded discovering human remains, and all they found was a hatchet. Or so at first they had thought. He really should tell the whole story to Greg. The whole point of Joachim's communication had been to lead them to those remains. That seemed no more far-fetched than any other explanation that occurred.

"I'm going out," he said to Phil as he emerged from his study.

"You just got home."

"I want to talk to Father Carmody."

"Use the phone."

"I want him to see this." Roger stuffed the diary into the pocket of his enormous jacket.

"He'll think you're crazy."

"Well, you already do."

Phil softened. "Want me to come with you?"

"One crazy brother in the family is enough."

He went out and got into his golf cart and started off. It was a crime not to be outside during this perfect autumn. The trees on campus, those along the road, were in glorious color. The conjunction of death and beauty was odd, but soon these lovely leaves would be lying lifeless on the ground, robbed of color, *les feuilles mortes*, being raked up, sucked into bags, ground almost to dust. Dust. The ultimate destiny of living things.

Autumn thoughts. Take any well-defined space, a campus, say, and think of the hundreds of dramas that had been enacted there. Thousands. More. Most of them concealed from the gaze of others. Even now, who knew what moral crises were forming among the students, the faculty, everyone connected with Notre Dame? Would any of them be entered enigmatically in diaries to confuse a fat former private investigator sometime in the future?

Father Carmody sat smoking in a chair outside the entrance. He looked up. Roger stopped and inhaled, acknowledging the aroma of the cigar.

"I am told that there is an ordinance against burning leaves," Father Carmody said.

"In South Bend."

"Did you have bonfires when you were a kid?"

"Phil and I had them until we came here."

"You want to talk."

166

"Finish your cigar."

Father Carmody got angrily to his feet. "I can smoke inside!"

Roger followed the priest inside; Father Carmody trailed a defiant cloud of smoke like a wood-burning locomotive of yore down the long corridor to his room. Once there, Roger had trouble extricating the diary from his pocket.

"What's that?"

Roger opened it to the page that had caught Greg Walsh's eye and handed the book to the priest.

Father Carmody read it standing; he looked at Roger, then sat down with a sigh. "Who else has seen this?"

"Greg Walsh."

"It has to go no farther. Will you agree to that?"

Roger had lowered himself onto the sofa, which was wide enough to accommodate him. "Certainly. And I'm sure you'll tell me why."

Father Carmody became lost in thought. He mumbled to himself as if involved in a debate. When it came to an end, he did not seem to like its outcome. "She told me in confidence. Not under the seal, but even so. Nonetheless, you have stumbled on this. Your curiosity is aroused. You will not let it go. You could stir up much unpleasantness."

Roger waited.

"Take a case. Two undergraduates, one male, one female, fall in love. They are not debauchees, but the flesh is weak. Do you follow me?"

Roger nodded.

"Debauchees would have taken what are called precautions. Of course this couple did not."

"She became pregnant."

"Exactly, and of course was surprised."

"And then?" Roger felt caught up in this, eager to hear what had happened next.

"A miscarriage. Not an abortion, a miscarriage."

"Infans sepelitur."

Roger's eyes misted as he imagined the scene, a distraught young woman, her previous dilemma giving way to this, a child who would never come to term. Had she been alone when she buried her inchoative child? Did he dare to put the question to Father Carmody? Clearly the priest was maneuvering through dangerous moral territory, saying as much as he had.

"Is this what Brother Joachim wanted us to know?" Roger asked.

"You may very well think so."

15   "SHE WAS PART OF THAT GROUP," Amanda said when Jay told her of the note he had received from Mame Childers. "Timothy Quinn and friends."

He should have remembered that. When he and his father had talked of those long-ago friends, the disappearing classmate, he had mentioned Mame, and Jay had asked if she was the girl all three of them had been after. A bad guess. "She was Casey's girl," his father had said. In her note, Mrs. Childers had made a lot of the fact that she and his father were old friends. Why didn't she just say class-mates? But then she had been a St. Mary's girl, not a Notre Dame student.

"The next time you're in New York, do come see me," she had written. "I am planning a little surprise for your father." Her address was on the Upper East Side.

"She's a client of mine," his father said when Jay asked who Mame Childers was. "Why do you ask about her?"

"I told you Larry Briggs mentioned her. Wasn't she a classmate of yours?" Acting dumb seemed the best course. He didn't want to spoil any surprise Mame Childers was planning for his father.

"Well, she was one of our bunch. On the edge of it, really."

"Where does she live?" Jay asked, being clever.

"New York." His father obviously didn't like this topic. "Jay, I may not have to let the condo on Longboat go."

"You're kidding."

"Finding a buyer has proved difficult."

"Dad, I'll buy it."

His father looked as if he were going to cry. "I appreciate it, Jay, but let's hold off on that. I may be able to hang on to it."

This was the most positive indication Jay had had that his father was in trouble. The poor guy. If Jay still missed his mother, how must his dad feel? Being a bachelor was one thing, but after you've had a wife and family, it must be really rough. Being clobbered by the market would make that loneliness even harder to bear. It occurred to Jay that he wasn't much support for his father.

"Maybe he'll marry again," Amanda said when he spoke of his dad's loneliness.

"Never!" What a crazy idea.

"Jay, how old is he? He's young. He's good-looking. Too bad it doesn't run in the family."

It was not the sort of thing he could ever joke about. The three of them. David, Bridget, Jay, had been drawn even closer together during his mother's last illness. He remembered when she had come home from Sloan-Kettering the final time. His dad had been told that nothing more could be done for her and was agonizing over whether to tell her that.

"Geez, don't do that, Dad."

"We always said we wouldn't keep that sort of thing a secret from one another."

"Would you want to be told there was no hope left for you?"

"Of course I would." He didn't sound like he meant it, though.

In the event, there had been no need to tell her. What else would she think when no further appointments had been made? At that time, she had only two weeks to live, and either Jay or his father was with her at all times. They were both there when she died, expelling a last breath that seemed to subside into a small guttural noise, then nothing. They had waited for her to take another breath, but there was only an eerie stillness. It was all over.

Jay had been a sophomore in high school at the time. He had never had to face anything that awful in his life before, but it was he who had to comfort his father. As they followed her casket down the aisle after her funeral Mass, his father had begun to weep uncontrollably, and Jay supported him out to the undertaker's limo.

In the following months, his father put in longer and longer hours at work. He looked like the wrath of God. Eventually his grief subsided, or he got it under control, and he and Jay did things together, ball games, movies, a raunchy Broadway musical. He was almost embarrassed by his father's laughter at all the smutty jokes. Still, it was probably good therapy. That closeness couldn't be kept up when Jay went off to South Bend. The two of them would have to do their grieving in private.

If nothing else, Mrs. Childers's note made him curious. He gave her a call and told her he would be in the city if she wanted to get together.

"Oh, how wonderful. Are you old enough to drink?"

"Hey."

She had in mind a bar and grill on Sixty-third. Could he find it?

"I'm an Eagle Scout."

"It'll be our secret."

When he arrived at the appointed time, she swept him into her arms, then stepped back, her hands on his upper arms. "His father's son," she said approvingly.

They were taken to a table off to the side, out of traffic. ("So we can talk.") She had a martini. He was about to order a beer, then changed it to bourbon and water. The only time he had drunk bourbon he had hated it. Amanda had told him it was an acquired taste. How do you acquire it? By being born Irish.

Mrs. Childers said, "I hated it when they banned smoking in bars."

"Do you smoke?"

"No. It's the principle of the thing. How wholesome this town has become. If you like fascism." She waved the topic away as an irrelevancy. "Tell me all about Notre Dame."

"You wouldn't recognize it now."

"That makes me sound awfully old."

"I'm quoting my father."

"How would he know what I would recognize?"

They got along just fine. She seemed younger than his father, acted younger, and she carried on as if this were a date of the other kind. Very flattering. He tried to imagine what she had looked like when she was his age.

"So what's the surprise?"

"My, you are direct."

She sat forward. "I have been to the condo on Longboat Key."

Jay put down his glass, remembering what his father had said. "It's on the market."

"Why else would Peaches show me the place?"

"Peaches?"

"Casey's wife." She stopped. "You're so much like your father I think we have the same memories. Casey Winthrop."

"The writer."

"Exactly."

"Have you read *Tumbleweed?*"

She hesitated. "Not yet."

"Amanda couldn't stand it."

"Amanda?" Her eyes widened. "Tell me all about Amanda."

"She's just a friend."

"That's the way it starts, Jay. Believe me, I know." She fell silent, ran a finger around the rim of her glass, seemed to decide not to go on.

"So what did you think of the condo?"

"I *love* it." Again she leaned forward. "Now for my secret."

She was all excited, telling him what she had told Peaches. "I meant it. Your father must not lose that place. It means too much to him."

"It means a lot to me, too."

"There you are! Your father must have told you he has suffered reversals of late. So have we all. But it would be madness for him to lose it."

"He would lose it if you bought it."

"Jay, darling. You're not paying attention. I don't want it for myself."

Jay was confused. How would it help his father if Mrs. Childers bought the condo on Longboat? She acted as if no explanation were necessary. Suddenly her gushing generosity irked him. Why should she interfere in his father's affairs?

"Well, enough of that. Now you know, and if you blab, I'll wring your neck. So tell me about Amanda."

"I'd rather talk about you. My dad said that you and Casey went together."

"Did he say that? Jay, it wasn't as if we were paired off. We couldn't have been; we were unbalanced. In every sense. Two girls, four boys. I went with your father as much as I did with Casey."

She got back to Amanda again, and he talked about the plan to revive Pelligrino's play *Behind the Bricks*.

"That's marvelous. We'll come see it."

"I'll keep you posted."

"I'll hate you if you don't."

Would he like another drink? Better not. He had proven to himself that he didn't like bourbon. It was half an hour later that they left. He hailed a cab for her, and before she got in, she kissed his cheek and said, "You're as much fun as your father."

He thought of that all the way back to Notre Dame.

16 WHO WAS IT THAT SAID THINGS HAP-
pen the first time as tragedy, the second time
as farce? Mame might have asked Dave, he knew such things, but
that was out. Besides, her failure to lure Dave away from Beth in the
dear long ago could hardly count as tragedy, and it was defeat she
was intent on avoiding now, not farce. For farcical she had Wilfrid
confronting Dave in his office, casting himself as the wronged husband! Only it wasn't funny. Mame was uneasily aware that any little
thing could send Dave out of her life forever.

"What in God's name did you have in mind, Will?"

She had found him at the Connecticut place, raking leaves from
under shrubs and hedges. Baggy suntans, a shapeless sweatshirt,
and those gunboat-sized XXL tennies could not turn Wilfrid into a
son of the soil. He looked like what he was, a Manhattan lawyer trying out for the Man with a Hoe. He tipped back the bill of his cap
and rubbed the tip of his nose, dumbfounded.

"You know what I'm talking about."

"Help me."

"Offering to open an account with Dave Williams."

"He wouldn't do it."

"Because he understood what you meant by it."

"Mame, I love you—"

"Oh, shut up."

She huffed down the path to her hideaway. Inside, she tossed her tote bag on a couch, circled her desk, and sat. Hands flat on the desk, eyes closed, she resolved that Dave's quoting Father Carmody would not be the trump card. How could he ignore Monsignor Sparrow's opinion? Mame was tired of waiting. She picked up the phone.

Dave called to ask her what the hell she was talking to his son about. He was angry. Mame liked that. Jay seemed another way to box Dave in. All's fair in adultery and war, but Mame wanted more. So did Dave, if he would only admit it. Mame was not at all impressed by his claim of undying devotion to his dead wife.

"You're as bad as Larry Briggs, Mame." There was something like contempt in his voice.

Mame and Philippa Briggs had lunched and talked about Larry. Even Philippa thought he had gone round the bend.

"Didn't Dave return his money, Flip?"

"Yes, and he sank it all into municipal bonds."

"So you're all right."

"All Larry talks about is what we would have had if Dave hadn't persuaded him to sell out. Mame, he's obsessed."

"Why don't you take a trip?"

"He has!"

"Alone."

Philippa pushed her glass away and hunched forward. "Believe me, I am enjoying a little peace and quiet."

"Where did he go?"

"He just took off." She sat back. "Did you know that you can take a steamboat on the Mississippi?"

"Is that what Larry is doing?"

"He wasn't sure what he was going to do. It was just one idea."

"Will isn't that wacko."

"What do you mean?

"Why does everyone hate Dave Williams?"

"Do you?"

Mame smiled. "Only every other day."

Mame might have told Dave about that luncheon conversation, but she didn't want to talk about Larry Briggs. She had half a mind to tell Dave that she was going out to see Father Carmody, but there was no need to play that card before she learned if it would win a trick. She hadn't a clue what the priest might say. In any case, her absence would go unnoticed by Dave when he finally decided to go to Kentucky and thank Pat Pelligrino for the money he had left him

17 ➤ THE NEWS FROM UP NORTH THREW
Casey off his writing schedule for several
days, off the project he was on, that is. He went back to the idea for
a novel that would incorporate the loss and reappearance of Timothy Quinn, Brother Joachim's odd bequest to David Williams, and
Beth Hanrahan up there in Minneapolis ladling out soup to the
scruffy images of God who showed up at Our Lady of the Road.

"How will you fit in?" Peaches asked. She was ripe as a melon
now, her due date just weeks away.

"Me? I'm the author."

"I meant back then."

"There were only three persons in the trinity, Peaches."

"Plus one Virgin Mary."

"Beth? Oh, she was something in those days. She could have
become an actress. She already was one."

"And you were just on the edge of it all?"

"Mame and I. That's how we ended up together."

"I don't want to hear it."

"Peaches, we were all different then."

Those long-ago events had been like the point in a novel toward
which everything converges; the point is reached, and the resulting
explosion provides the denouement, scattering them all. Not that he
would put it like that to Peaches. He hated blathering about the art

of writing. People write a novel or two and suddenly they're experts about the craft of fiction. Meaning they can tell you how they themselves did it, if that. Do magicians go around explaining their tricks? He shouldn't have said that about Mame.

Dave Williams's decision to take his condo off the market hadn't exactly blighted Peaches's day. She had tons of listings, showings every day, but not many deals were closed. Buyers were always putting off decisions, hoping prices would keep dropping, and owners were skittish. Almost none of them wanted to sell. Selling represented defeat, the admission that affluence had turned into its opposite. Dave was lucky to have been bailed out by Pat Pelligrino.

Dave had always been lucky. Despite the stiff competition, he had ended up with Beth, something Casey found out about quite by accident. How many guys would have had the guts to ask for the use of a room? Back then, they were all pretty decent. Read about campuses now, and they sound like nonstop Roman orgies. Overstated, no doubt, but the whole attitude toward sex had changed, and for the worst. No wonder people turned to Jane Austen for relief. That was the attraction of Westerns for Casey. Strong macho heroes and women who were the kind of women their mothers had been. You want the other kind, go downtown to the saloon. Of course it was a formula, as old as fiction. A woman attracts a man; obstacles arise and have to be confronted one by one. The efforts bring about a series of failures, everything looks bleak, and then our hero comes plausibly through against great odds, he folds the woman in his arms, and the sun sinks slowly in the west. You couldn't write such stories if you didn't believe in them. Peaches's condition brought back another memory.

How many times had Dave asked to use his room before it just stopped? Something had happened. In retrospect, he could imagine that he had suspected something, that he had noticed a change in Beth. Pregnant? My God. What had happened to the baby, if there had been one? It would have been unthinkable for Beth to have an abortion.

"What did you mean, you and Mame ended up together?"

"I thought you didn't want to know."

"Maybe you want to get it off your chest."

"Have you ever thought of writing fiction?"

He took her on his lap, not as easy an operation now, and pressed her cheek to his. It was better than a Western.

Mame. The last time she was down she had stopped by, asking for Peaches, but she must have known she would be at the office or on the job, showing places to prospective buyers. Mame strolled around his work area, fluttering pages, peering at the computer screen, then went to the shelf where his books were arrayed and began counting them.

"Don't."

"How many are there?"

"That's most of them."

"But not all?"

"When a paperback's shelf life is over, you don't have much chance of finding a copy."

Once, against his rules, he had spoken to a meeting of used book dealers and had begun by announcing that it had always been his ambition to write used books. They had loved it. So had he. It was true, too. All he really wanted was readers, but you never know your readers. It was a weird life.

"You are amazing, Casey," Mame said.

"I've forgotten how to blush modestly."

"Dave said to me that sometimes he thought he was the only one of us who ended up living a normal life. He forgot about you."

"You call this normal?"

"I call it wonderful."

The thing about Mame, she never let you forget that she was a woman and you were a man. The outfit she wore involved nine colors at least, and she came on like a rainbow. It had the kind of skirt that swirled every chance it got. The big plastic belt emphasized Mame's slenderness. Or maybe it was the contrast with Peaches.

"All this and Peaches, too," Mame said.

"Maybe I should start buying lottery tickets."

"Dave and I are not going to marry." Just like that, out of the blue. Casey just stared. "Did you know Bridget?"

"A little. Not really."

"He's still in love with her."

"Tough for you?"

"Casey, have you ever really tried to recall those years when we were all on campus? I mean really bring it all back. It wasn't very flattering to have the three of them nuts about Beth."

"You had me."

She smiled. "Did I?"

"So you and Dave aren't going to get married."

"Who told you that?"

"You did."

She thought. "That's right, I did. It just slipped out."

He had little doubt that it was an announcement of something else. Peaches had said that Mame was still nuts about Dave, talked about nothing else. For crying out loud, she had wanted to buy his condo so he wouldn't lose it. It sounded like something in the kind of novel he no longer cared to write.

"A funny thing. Dave says that when Beth got back to Minneapolis, Timothy was no longer there. Vamoosed."

"I suppose he got used to being lost."

It was several days later that Tim showed up. Bearded, open road, open sky, king of the road. Casey didn't recognize him at first and figured he had come for a handout.

"I recognize you," the man said.

Casey peered at him through the screen. My God. "Tim?"

Of course he asked him in. Casey offered to make lunch.

"Anything but soup."

Tim told him about taking off from Minneapolis before Beth got back from Notre Dame.

"Just took off?"

"It's my signature move."

Casey thought about that. "How was the army?"

"You're kidding."

"I thought you were antiwar."

"What's that got to do with being a GI?"

There they were, talking away as if two decades hadn't intervened, Casey not yet the fiction machine and Tim not yet the mystery man whose signature move was just to take off.

"Where are you going?"

"I've been. Do you know how long a drive it is from Minneapolis?"

Casey groaned in sympathy. Beth had an old car, a gift, but still in good shape. Actually the thought of getting behind the wheel and setting off for nowhere in particular suddenly had an enormous appeal. Let the computer cool off, recharge the old batteries. Nonsense, of course. Tim didn't have a Peaches to anchor him.

"You've been working with Beth?"

"It's not work."

"How is she?"

"The same and different. Like everybody else." Tim spoke in almost dreamy tones.

"Still nuts about her?"

No need to answer. Tim just looked around Casey's workroom. "You ever see Dave Williams?"

"Once in a while."

"You know he got Beth pregnant."

"Come on."

"It's true. She lost the baby. I stopped at Gethsemani on the way down to see Pat. We talked of little else."

"Geez."

"I could have killed him. Pat felt the same way." A pause. "Pat got over it."

Casey did not pursue the implications of that.

"Beth's painting his picture."

Tim made it sound like a crime. Dave called her up after who knows how many years and the first thing she did was get out photographs and set up her easel.

"She paints?"

"She still loves him."

"No harm in that. Have they gotten together?"

"No!"

"Dave and Mame seem to be going together."

"Isn't he married?"

"A widower. His boy is a student at Notre Dame."

"How old are your kids?"

"There's only one. Minus one month old." He had to explain it. "How did you get here, Tim?"

"Drove. I'll stop in Kentucky to see Brother Joachim again on the way back."

"I've always wanted to do that."

"They will welcome you like Christ himself. It's in their rule."

"What did he make of recent developments?"

"Pat? Oh, he's floated free of all that. I asked him why the hell he had dumped all that money on David Williams."

"And?"

"He said he might have given it to me but he thought I was dead. What a sonofabitch."

"Pat?"

"Dave Williams. When Beth fell for him I got out. Like Pat, I thought of killing him first, but what good would that have done?"

"Dave? None."

"Beth wouldn't talk to me for days after I told her that."

He was restless while he ate and afterward shuffled around. "Well, I'll be off."

"Wait and meet Peaches."

"Peaches?"

"My wife."

Tim stared at him. "So you're doing okay?"

"I'm doing okay."

"What do you do?"

"Do?"

"What kind of work?"

"My wife works."

Afterward he was glad Tim hadn't stayed to meet Peaches. Where was he going?

Tim wasn't sure. Just going. "I suppose I'll go back to Minneapolis eventually."

"Good idea."

He didn't tell Peaches about the visit.

He hadn't told her that Mame had dropped by, either.

18 AMANDA ZIKOWSKI FOUND THE STORY involving Jay's father more interesting than he did, apparently. After the first burst of publicity—for a week there had been follow-ups of the original story in the campus publications, but then they stopped—Jay seemed annoyed at her continuing interest. How could she be interested in the past when there was this wonderful present containing him? Well, males grow up more slowly than females, she knew that, but what a romantic glow was cast over the campus by those long-ago dramatic events. Three men and one woman and all the interesting things they had done. Amanda went to the archives, where Greg Walsh found a copy of Patrick Pelligrino's play *Behind the Bricks.* It seemed to foreshadow what was to happen. A bright golden moment, that group illumining the campus with their acitivities, and then one of them, Timothy Quinn, mysteriously disappeared. Now, two decades later, it turned out that he had been alive all along.

The archivist let Amanda photocopy the script, and she tried to interest Jay in it. "A revival, Jay. Think of it."

"A revival implies that something was once alive."

"Oh, Jay."

"Casey Winthrop is the most interesting one of the whole damned bunch. My dad thinks so, too. Have you read *Tumbleweed?*"

"A Western? You're not serious."

"We should invite him to campus to talk about his work."

"Jay, he writes paperbacks."

"Readable paperbacks. What a sense of story."

He was serious. "Okay. I'll go along with you if you go along with me."

That became their agreement. She helped him write a letter of invitation to Casey Winthrop, editing out his claim that his books were all the rage on campus—there wasn't a single title available in the bookstore—and offering an honorarium of a thousand dollars, plus travel, etc.

"Where are we going to get a thousand dollars?" Amanda wanted to know.

"I'll donate it."

He had told her that his mother had left him money, and she had resisted asking how much. Well, it didn't have to be a fortune to enable him to come up with the honorarium and expenses. They walked to the post office and sent off the letter.

"He won't accept," Jay said.

"You can't know that."

"Given his productivity, he must never leave his computer." He asked his father if he would put in a word for them anyway and came back with the story of Peaches.

"Peaches!"

"His wife. She's expecting. She's a child bride, much younger than he is."

"What's her real name?"

"Why not Peaches?"

"You couldn't baptize a child Peaches."

"I never tried."

As she had feared, he dragged his feet when she turned their attention to putting on *Behind the Bricks*. Amanda wanted an amateur group and somewhere other than Washington Hall, although that was where the play had been put on before. There was a stage in the auditorium of the Hesburgh Center.

The manager thought they were kidding when they asked about putting on a play there. "It's an auditorium, not a theater."

"We've looked it over. It would be perfect."

The manager let his head roll from side to side. "Look, you check at McKenna, and if they give it a go-ahead, okay."

It took two days to get through the red tape. The initial answer was no, absolutely not, but the woman who said this seemed to find Jay interesting, so Amanda let him do the talking. All three of them went over to Hesburgh to look at the auditorium.

"Impossible." Her name was Hazel, and she seemed to hope her negatives would get a rise out of Jay.

"Did you ever see Thornton Wilder's *Our Town*?"

Hazel hadn't.

"Minimalist settings. You enlist the imaginations of the audience." Jay paused and studied Hazel. "Have you ever acted?"

"Me!" she giggled, putting a hand over her ample bosom.

Jay turned to Amanda. "What do you think?"

"You're the producer."

"I think you'd be perfect for the second lead."

Did he mean the character that bricked up the victim? Hazel was flattered, but she wasn't insane. They went back to her office, and she pulled out forms, continuing to say that there was no way in which this could be done.

It was done. Before leaving, Jay asked Hazel if she was a senior. She inflated in indignation. "A senior?"

"A graduate student?"

"Get out of here."

"You're shameless," Amanda said when they were outside.

"You have to understand the feminine psyche."

"Ha."

"I thought she was kind of cute. Sweat off a hundred pounds or so . . ."

"We'll need a third."

"Whoa. One Hazel is enough."

"A third actor. You and I and who?"

"How about Roger Knight?"

"Have you written any good poems lately?"

"I don't write good poems."

She told Roger Knight their plans after his next seminar. Jay had stopped coming after having failed to discredit the Huneker Professor of Catholic Studies, whom he now referred to as Sherlock.

"Greg Walsh told me you had been asking about the play."

"Oh, you know him."

"He's one of my best friends."

Why should she be surprised? A stammering archivist and a three-hundred-pound professor. She also told him about the invitation to Casey Winthrop.

He was delighted. "I have been toying with the idea of devoting a semester to Notre Dame authors."

"Do you know what he writes?"

"I am one of his most devoted fans."

Amanda gave up. She had tried to read *Tumbleweed* but hadn't made it to chapter three.

Some days later an excited Jay told her that Casey Winthrop had responded to their letter with a phone call. "He said he never gives talks."

"Oh, well."

"Of course he wanted to be persuaded. So I persuaded him. All we have to do is settle on a date."

"Hazel will veto it." Hazel seemed to control the use of all the campus buildings.

"My dear, you underestimate my persuasiveness." He closed his eyes. "Moonlight can be so cruelly deceptive."

"Who are you imitating?"

"Noël Coward?"

19 ⟶ MAME CHILDERS, NÉE SAYERS, WAS
the picture of affluent sophistication, the kind
of woman Father Carmody did not like, but then he hadn't liked her
as a student either. When she called from the Morris Inn to ask him
to dinner, his first impulse was to say no. Not because of her. He
realized that he was no longer patient with unforeseen disruptions
of the even tenor of his ways. If he didn't know himself better, he
would think he was getting old. He accepted her invitation, but with
foreboding.

She rose from a lobby chair when he came into the Morris Inn
and swept toward him with a radiant smile. There was no way of
avoiding her embrace. He felt enveloped in the invisible cloud of her
perfume.

"Father, what is your secret? You don't look a day older."

"Just years older?"

She actually squeezed his arm. "I have been sitting here wondering how long it has been she we were last together."

The suggestion that this was the resumption of a warm friendship
did not improve his disposition. He told her that the last time she
saw him must have been 1989.

"Shhh," she said. Another squeeze.

Into the dining room then, Sorin's, where Mame posed by the
receptionist desk, keeping a grip on his arm. As they were led to

their table, Father Carmody did not look around, not wanting to know who might be witnesses of this grand entrance.

He declined a drink when the question was put to them, and Mame protested. "I want this to be a celebration."

"Of what?"

She looked mysterious. "Later."

"I never drink." It seemed a pardonable exaggeration.

"Then I won't either."

"Nonsense. Have something."

"Well . . ."

While they waited for her martini to arrive, she sat across from him, smiling possessively.

"Tell me what we're celebrating."

She hesitated, then opened her purse and took out an envelope, which she handed to him. He recognized the name of the Manhattan parish.

"What's this?"

"It's from Monsignor Sparrow." A pause. "My pastor."

"Aha. You plan to enter the convent."

She stared at him, then burst into laughter.

Father Carmody opened the envelope and took out the letter, surprised to find that it was addressed to him. He read it, read it again. Monsignor Sparrow informed Father Carmody, somewhat officiously, that there were no canonical impediments to Mame's marrying again.

"Again?"

Her drink came. She lifted it in a toast, and he raised his glass of water.

"Why don't I just review the whole thing, Father."

So he heard of her marriage to Wilfrid, a wonderful man in many ways, and they continued to have the highest respect for one another, despite the differences in their outlook on life. She looked at him significantly.

"He isn't a Catholic, Father. We weren't married in the Church." She adopted a naughty little girl expression.

"Any children?"

She looked away for a moment. "That was one of the differences."

"So you divorced."

"We divorced. So much you will have heard from David Williams."

"David Williams?"

"Father, you remember the group of us here. We seem to be back in the news again. Isn't it astounding that Timothy Quinn has been alive all along? Anyway, David has been my financial adviser in recent years. We realized that even after the passage of time there remained an attraction." She stopped, and her expression became sorrowful. "Why did you tell him I cannot marry again?"

Suddenly the letter from Monsignor Sparrow began to make sense. In it he seemed to be reproving Father Carmody for his deficient knowledge of canon law.

"You want to marry again?"

She pursed her lips. "You're teasing. I know Dave has spoken with you."

They were interrupted by the waitress, thank God, and went about the business of ordering. This gave Father Carmody time to realize the position he was in. Mame, the affluent divorcée, and David Williams, widower, had been thrown together in the fleshpots of Manhattan. Whatever their relationship, Mame interpreted it as the prelude to marriage. For all Father Carmody knew, Dave had proposed to her, but it was equally clear that Dave had used him as an excuse for not going ahead with it. The problem this posed was a difficult one, but one that had its attractions for a man who had spent so many years in the devious ways of administration. Of course, he could simply blurt out that he knew nothing about it, that he had never discussed the matter with David Williams, nor vice versa, to make that crystal clear, but that simple path did not appeal.

"What does David make of the monsignor's judgment?"

"He invokes your veto."

He sipped his water. "Veto is a little strong."

"Oh, I am so glad to hear you say that."

"Canon law was never my strongest suit."

"But Dave said you were so positive."

"It's my manner, I suppose."

They were served and for some minutes busied themselves with food. But already Mame was aglow with relief. The supposed veto of Father Carmody was not as firm as she assumed.

Anyone in authority must learn that, while always telling the truth, he is not obliged to tell the whole truth to every party. This carries with it the note of dissembling and can easily lead into outright duplicity. Father Carmoldy could cite instances. There was no need to tell Mame that he had never discussed a possible marriage with David. He was already looking forward to talking with David about this amazing conversation.

"He has been your financial adviser?"

"Yes."

"These have been difficult economic times."

"I have lost money, yes. Is there anyone who hasn't? Of course David feels very badly about it. Not that I am stony broke, far from it, but he takes personal responsibility for the recession. He has even offered to reimburse me the amount I lost."

Ah. The bequest from Brother Joachim. The Trappist alumnus

was a useful diversion, and Father Carmody went on about that. "You mentioned your group. There is also Beth Hanrahan. Have you kept in touch with her?"

"Hardly. She has become a saint."

That was not how Beth would have described herself, but doubtless Beth's selfless life in Minneapolis would suggest heroic virtue to a Manhattanite.

They got through the meal without any need for Father Carmody to tell an outright falsehood. Except about never drinking. In recompense he joined Mame in a brandy when the table was cleared.

"I've been told it is a tasty drink."

"Father, I can't tell you the trepidation I felt coming to you like this. I had no idea how I could broach the subject."

"Monsignor Sparrow's letter did that."

"Didn't it? I'll say it again. I am so relieved. Will you talk to David?"

He pretended to hesitate. "Yes," he said. "I will talk to David."

He suffered another embrace and another envelopment in perfume. When he went out to his car, he was rather pleased with himself. He would have called his performance jesuitical, except that he knew too many Jesuits.

20 JAY WILLIAMS SAT IN LEAHY'S
Lounge in the Morris Inn across a little table
from Mrs. Childers, who had surprised him with her call, telling
him that she was on campus and hoped they could get together.
With the egoism of youth, he assumed she had flown to South Bend
just to see him. Ever since their meeting in New York, he had been
puzzling about what she had said then. Once he got out from under
the zillion-kilowatt floodlight of her sophisticated charm he had
found himself strangely depressed. It was her possessive attitude
toward his father and her zany notion that she would buy the condo
on Longboat Key so his father wouldn't lose it that had been her big
surprise. If she bought it, though, she would own it, not his father.

"Bourbon and water?" she asked Jay when Murph the bartender
came for their orders.

"Beer."

Her elegant eyebrows lifted, but she said nothing. "Martini," she
told Murph.

She had slipped off her coat and draped it over the back of her
chair. Now she drew it over her shoulders. "It's chilly in here."

"My dad has taken the condo off the market."

"Isn't that wonderful?"

"You knew that?"

"Of course." She seemed to be reading his thoughts. "Casey

Winthrop's wife is the Realtor in the case. Peaches." A little laugh. "Only in Florida. I suppose it might have been Oranges."

"Have you had a chance to get around the campus?"

"Oh, this is just an in-and-out trip. Do you know Father Carmody?"

"I've heard of him."

"He was such a power, Jay. The man behind the throne. It is painful to think of him filed away in Holy Cross House."

"You've seen him."

"That was the point of the exercise." A hand fluttered out and rested on his. "And to see you, of course. I want us to be friends."

He fought the surge of pleasure. Of course she was nuts about him, what else? Middle-aged woman makes fool of herself over Notre Dame undergraduate. Thomas Wolfe had had an older mistress.

"I had hoped you'd bring Amanda."

"She's all wrapped up in the revival of Pelligrino's play."

"Of course."

"It's a lousy play."

"I always thought so. Still, it was so much fun putting it on. Dave was such a good actor."

Dave. Well, what the hell, they had gone to school together—but that was a long time ago.

"Why did you have to see Father Carmody, Mrs. Childers?"

Murph brought the drinks, and she fell silent until he left them. "I'll let your father tell you."

His father! He pushed away the glass Murph handed him and brought the bottle to his lips. She followed this as if he were performing some Olympic event, smiling wondrously.

"I haven't drunk beer from the bottle since . . ." She pursed her lips and half turned her head, her eyes never leaving him. "But there. I sound like an old woman."

"You're not an old woman."

Not at all, my dear, What's a decade or two difference in age? They can be erased by the ardor of our love. I will make you young again.

"Thank you. And stop calling me Mrs. Childers, please. It's Mame."

"Is Mame short for something?"

She laughed. "Does it sound like Peaches to you?"

Banter. Persiflage. Repartee. Bullshit. As he talked with her, playing the Ping-Pong of patter, saying what you don't mean and meaning what you don't say, the depression he had felt after their meeting in New York put in a reappearance. What were his plans for Thanksgiving? "I plan to be with my father." She acted as if she had already known that. He was relieved when the flunky looked in the door of the bar and told her her cab had come.

She gave a little cry and got to her feet. He held her coat so she could get her arms into the sleeves. On the way out, she put money on the counter, twice what the drinks cost, and sailed out. Her bags were being put into the cab when they went outside and stood under the canopy. She turned to Jay, a look of pained pleasure on her perfect face, then gathered him into his arms. Her lips pressed his cheek. She stepped into the cab and looked up at him.

"Wipe that off your cheek, Jay. Amanda will be furious."

The door was pulled shut, a flutter of her hand, and the taxi moved away. The doorman smiled at Jay.

"Your mother?"

"No!"

The doorman's expression changed. He actually winked. Jay got the hell out of there.

————

That night, late, he got his father on his cell phone. "Is this a good time?"

"I'm at dinner, but go ahead."

Jay could hear the sounds of a restaurant now. "It's nothing important. Mrs. Childers was out here today."

Silence. "You don't say."

"We had a drink in the Morris Inn."

He could hear voices, too, and then one distinctive voice, apparently speaking to the waiter. Mame Childers? Jay pushed the OFF button and sat staring at the wall of his room. His cell phone rang. He didn't answer.

That night he dreamt of his mother. The dream woke him up, it was so vivid. He got out of bed, quietly, not wanting to wake his roommates. He sat up in the dark and tried not to think. Easier said than done. His mother's face swam before him, he had carried the sound of her voice from his dream, and then he thought of Mame Childers. What an idiot he was. It seemed obvious now what she had been trying to tell him without actually saying it. So of course she wanted them to be friends.

Don't act like a kid, he told himself. *Grow up.* As Amanda had said, his father was still a young man. It was really trading down to turn to someone like Mame, but what the hell? She was fun, she was . . . He was almost surprised to find that he was crying, sitting there in the darkened dorm room, weeping like a baby, feeling that his father was betraying his mother. He remembered sparring with his father, just kidding around, pulling their punches. When he went back to his bed he drove his fist into his pillow. The sonofabitch!

Well, he could celebrate Thanksgiving by himself.

21 PEACHES WAS AS BIG AS A HOUSE, but she still had a fortnight or so to go. Twins? They had both nixed the notion of a scan. That had been proposed earlier to determine the sex of the child.

"I want to be surprised," Casey said. "Like Adam."

"Didn't Eve have twins?"

"I'll look it up. Better yet, I'll ask Brother Joachim."

He loved it when she squinted, making little chevrons appear on her forehead. What a blessing she was. For years he had thought he was a celibate.

"What's that?" Peaches had asked. Chevrons then, too.

"Sort of like a reprobate."

Now she said, "What do you mean, you'll ask Brother Joachim?"

"I'm thinking of a little research trip. For the new novel."

"You'll have to go alone."

"It will only be for a few days."

He drove, up through Atlanta, Chattanooga, and Nashville into Kentucky. Signs indicating Civil War sites flashed by. See the country by interstate. He might still be on I-75. He found the monastery without a hitch.

When he told a monk in the guesthouse that he had come to see an old Notre Dame classmate, the monk said, "Joachim?"

"You know him?" Casey paused. "Dumb question."

"You're his second visitor today."

Casey looked at the monk. "Maybe I'd better wait." He looked around the guesthouse lobby. Maybe he could stay here.

"Perhaps you know him. David Williams."

"Of course I know him. We were classmates."

"It could be a class reunion." The monk smiled. "My father taught at Notre Dame."

Chadwick, Chadwick? Casey pretended to recognize the name.

"Joachim is out in the hermitage. I'll take you there."

"Couldn't I find it myself?"

"Probably."

"You better show me."

It was odd to be back where there are seasons. Many leaves had fallen, but the trees were bright with the colors of autumn. He asked Brother Chrysologus if he had gone to Notre Dame. He had. If Casey had expected a flow of reminiscence he would have been disappointed. Ten minutes later, Chrysologus stopped and pointed. Casey had trouble seeing the hermitage.

"I never would have found it."

"Probably not."

It was a low wooden cottage with a front porch on which a rocker moved slightly in the breeze.

"What does he do out here?"

"He's on retreat."

Retreat from the monastery? Chrysologus gave a piercing whistle as they approached the hermitage. No answer. Onto the porch then, and Chysologus knocked on the door before opening it. Or trying to open it. There was something preventing this.

"Chrysologus?"

Another monk came toward them around the house, apparently emerging from the woods. He stopped when he came closer and smiled. "Casey?"

It was Joachim. Casey had difficulty recognizing him, but maybe that was a two-way street. How do you greet a monk? Casey took his hand; he took both his hands. "Is Dave Williams here?"

"Inside."

Chrysologus said, "The door is stuck. I tried it."

Joachim went around his brother monk and tried the door as Chrysologus had. He managed to open it a bit, then put his head in and looked around. Suddenly he backed away, put his shoulder to the door, and drove through. Casey and Chrysologus followed him in.

The body lay on the floor, arms outstretched, an ugly wound on the head, blood from it trickling down Dave Williams's cheek. Joachim was on his knees and began to murmur a prayer.

As if in answer, there was a guttural groan from Williams. Joachim turned to Chrysologus. "The infirmarian, Brother."

Chrysologus nodded, pounded across the porch, and jogged off in the direction of the monastery.

22 THE INFIRMARY WAS NOT A LARGE
room, but the high windows, the white walls,
and the beds with their white spreads gave an air of spaciousness.
On one wall was a huge crucifix, very realistic, with great nails in the
body, the crown of thorns huge and ugly, the wounds running with
brightly painted blood. Brother Bernard, the infirmarian, came and
went, seeming to follow his smile in and out of the room. Dave Williams
looked like a monk himself, a sleeping monk, lying there with
a white sheet to his chin, his head shaved, wearing a white turbanlike
bandage, a pale face on the white pillow, out of the world.

Bernard looked at Casey when he asked when he could speak to
Dave. "He's in a coma, son."

Brother Bernard's specialty in what he called the world had been
brain surgery. "Here we do soul surgery."

"So you're an MD."

"For my sins. I was on the staff of the Mayo Clinic."

"How long have you been a monk?"

"Not long enough."

"Did you have to shave Dave's head?"

"I wanted to make him feel at home."

Bernard kept shining lights in Dave's eyes, humming as he did so.

"How long do comas last?"

"Why don't we leave that in the hands of God?"

The infirmary was state-of-the-art, and Bernard was more than competent; it wasn't that he meant to just stand by and watch. Hours later, Dave was in an ambulance, being taken to the nearest MRI. Bernard wanted a brain scan. It showed extensive damage to the brain. Surgery? Bernard shook his head slowly.

Casey was anxious to get back to Peaches. He explained why to Bernard.

"Your friend could linger for, who knows how long? You should go home to your wife."

He wanted to talk to Joachim before leaving. What had happened to Dave? Both Joachim and Chrysologus had reacted calmly and efficiently in the crisis. Joachim's first impulse had been to send Dave shriven into eternity, but after the groan indicated that he was still alive and Chrysologus loped off to get the infirmarian, Casey and Joachim lifted Dave from the floor and put him on the cot in the hermitage bedroom. Over the inert body, Casey asked, "What happened?"

Joachim turned eyes that were like mirrors at him, then shook his head. "He was attacked."

"By whom?"

"We had been sitting, talking. About old times. Notre Dame. I had left him alone there, going to say my rosary. I wasn't away five minutes when I heard Chrysologus whistle."

It was difficult to face Joachim when the doubts started. The hermitage was an isolated place; there had been only Joachim and Dave. In profile, Joachim still looked like Pat Pelligrino, his old classmate, no one who would attack another person.

"Did you see anyone else?"

A shake of the head. Silence. "Do you think I did it, Casey?"

"Of course not!" But he looked away when he said it.

They sat by the cot in silence then, waiting for Chrysologus and the infirmarian. Dave's breathing was audible in the little room. Listening, Casey thought that was what the blow had been meant to stop, Dave's breathing. Someone had tried to kill him. Chrysologus's whistle might have saved his life.

Chrysologus had returned to the hermitage with Bernard and four other monks, and after a preliminary examination the infirmarian ordered Dave taken to the infirmary. Four monks lifted the cot with Dave on it and maneuvered it outside. Getting out of their way, Casey noticed the back door of the hermitage. They returned to the monastery, an odd procession, Bernard first, then the cot, followed by Casey and Joachim.

Casey had never seen anyone die before. He had killed off dozens of characters in his books, but death in fiction is not the real thing. The real thing took place in the infirmary. Casey had been sitting there, hoping Dave would come out of his coma, when Dave's breathing became erratic. Bernard came and did the work of a priest, anointing Dave. Joachim arrived, and Chrysologus. The intervals between the breaths lengthened, and when the next one came it seemed miraculous. Then Dave breathed what turned out to be his last. They all seemed to be waiting for another, but another never came. The monks began to chant in Latin.

The abbot had arrived in time to see Dave die. He seemed to think that Casey had come to make a retreat.

Casey felt guilty about being so eager to leave the monastery and get home to Peaches—but, good God, what if she went into labor while he was away? The solution seemed to be to call Notre Dame. Father Carmody, at Joachim's suggestion.

When on the third try Casey got through to Father Carmody— the Notre Dame switchboard seemed something out of a Marx Brothers movie—he had his message compressed and ready to go.

"Father, this is Casey Winthrop, Class of '89. I'm calling from Gethsemani, the Trappist monastery in Kentucky. Dave Williams, my classmate, is here. In the infirmary. Someone attacked him."

He had to parse each sentence and expand on it before Carmody got it. "The infirmary?"

"Yes."

"Attacked?"

"Hit over the head. In the hermitage. He was visiting Brother Joachim, another classmate."

"How serious is it?"

"Father, he's dead."

How easy that was to say. There was a silence.

"And what are you doing there, Casey?"

"Making a retreat."

Or intending to make one. Or lying. He told Father Carmody he had to get back to his wife in Florida.

"I can get in touch with you there?"

He gave him his cell number as well as the number at the house.

"Class of '89?"

"Yes, Father."

A pause. Then, "Okay. Thank you, Casey. Have a safe trip home." He had seemed about to say something else.

———

Driving a long distance is a contemplative act, particularly on the interstate. Casey kept remembering the back door of the hermitage. A scenario began to take shape in his mind; think of it as a draft for a novel. Dave Williams comes to see his old classmate Pat Pelligrino, now Brother Joachim. They are sitting on the porch, talking about old times, talking about Notre Dame. That sounded peaceful enough. But he was remembering as well what he had heard of the packet Joachim had sent to the Notre Dame archives, stirring up old memories, claiming Timothy Quinn, who it turned out was still alive, had been killed. Joachim had also left Dave a pile of money. Why Dave? *Why not me, for crying out loud?*

In the scenario, the two men in the hermitage began to argue; they stood; Joachim went outside, picking up a piece of firewood, which he brought down on Dave's head. Joachim hears a whistle. He pulls the door shut behind him, beats it out the back way, and comes around the hermitage to greet Chrysologus and Casey.

By the time he got to Atlanta, Casey had touched it up, tightened it. Going through Valdosta, he was reciting it as if it were an eyewitness report. On the long plumb line of I-75, dropping through Florida, his speed matching the number of the road, he insisted to himself that he was writing fiction in his head. An occupational hazard. Finally, he just wanted to get back to Peaches and forget the whole damned thing.

23 "WAS HE BADLY HURT?" ROGER ASKED when Father Carmody came by to tell them about David Williams.

"They got him to the infirmary. He died there," the old priest said, unzipping his jacket. Outside the weather had turned from golden autumn to early winter, the wind whipping leaves from the trees and sending them cartwheeling over the lawn. "One of the monks is a doctor. I hope you have coffee."

They had coffee. Phil brought Father Carmody a brimming mug. He dipped into it immediately, looking at the two brothers over the rim. He sat back then, shivering. "I'm getting too old for this kind of weather."

Father Carmody told the story at his own pace. He had received a call from Casey Winthrop, another member of the Class of 1989 who happened to be visiting the monastery. "Happened," he repeated. "He went out to the hermitage with another monk, Emil Chadwick's son, and they discovered the body. Joachim had been out in the woods, saying the rosary, taking a break from reminiscing about their time here."

It was impossible for any of them to think about what had happened in Kentucky without connecting it to the odd events of recent weeks: Joachim's package to the archives, the reappearance of Timothy Quinn, and of course the great revelation of the burial that had been made near the Log Chapel, Patrick Pelligrino helping Beth Hanrahan inter her stillborn child. *Infans sepelitur.*

"I want you to go down there, Phil," Father Carmody said. "I talked with the abbot and asked him to consider the hermitage as a crime scene. No one to go near the place until you get there."

That suggested that he considered his request answered in the affirmative, but Phil did not quarrel with that.

"I'll go with you," Roger said.

"Of course."

Father Carmody seemed surprised. "Is that necessary, Roger?"

"Not in a strict logical sense, if the necessary is that which cannot not be. Call it hypothetical necessity."

The old priest went back to his coffee. He had spent his whole life on campus, save for some years in Rome, but he was still impatient with academic niceties and distinctions.

Roger reminded him that Thanksgiving was coming up, so he wouldn't be skipping more than a class or two, and he could make those up in evening meetings when he came back. "It will give the students time to read *On the Soul.*"

Neither Phil nor Father Carmody commented on this. Roger chided himself. Was he becoming pedantic?

Father Carmody's concern was who should be informed of what had happened to David Williams. "The abbot was pretty unexcited about what had occurred."

"Considering it *sub specie aeternitatis?*"

"Aquinas?"

"Actually Spinoza. An interesting name. Of course you know what it means?"

"Roger!" Phil said.

The priest said, "Williams is a widower. His son is a student here."

"I know him," Roger said.

"I don't want to alarm the boy. We're only dealing with hearsay and at a distance. I suppose it's against the rule for a Trappist to get excited."

"If his father is in the infirmary, you can tell him that," Roger said.

"You want to call him?"

Roger picked up the Notre Dame directory and began to flip through its pages. When he found what he was looking for, he reached for the phone.

"What are you going to tell him?"

"I'll play it by ear. What else is a telephone for?"

Father Carmody held out his mug to Phil. "You got anything to put in this?"

"Courvoisier."

"No need to dilute that."

Roger listened to the ringing of Jay Williams's phone. After five rings, he hung up. "How often is a student in his room?"

"There used to be an answer to that," Father Carmody said, taking the bulbous glass of amber liquid Phil gave him. "To a happy death," he said, lifting it.

Roger went back to the directory, then dialed again. This time he was lucky. "Amanda? This is Roger Knight. I wonder if you could get a message to Jay Williams."

"We're not speaking."

Roger hesitated. He remembered Amanda telling him that Jay was miffed because she wasn't casting him in the revival of Pelligrino's *Behind the Bricks*: "He couldn't act his way out of a wet paper bag. He can't be convincing. Of course he thinks it's a lousy play." Now Roger said, "Couldn't you just deliver a message? I'd like him to call me."

"Maybe he'll write you a poem."

The battle between the sexes was a mystery to Roger. The attractions and repulsions of the genders, the touchiness alternating with tenderness, were as foreign to him as the alleged antics in Samoa. "You'll tell him?"

"You could leave a message on his phone."

Roger realized that he hadn't waited long enough to be told to begin his message when he heard the beep.

"Oh, I'll tell him," Amanda said. "I haven't had a good fight all day."

When he had replaced the phone, Father Carmody went on. "Imagine the probability of two members of the class of 1989 being at a Trappist abbey at the same time."

"Three," Roger corrected. "Brother Joachim."

"Touché."

"We'll leave in the morning," Phil said.

The brandy had taken away Father Carmody's chill. He took off his jacket now and settled back. "Now who do you suppose would want to hit David Williams over the head with a stick of firewood?"

"That was the weapon?"

"So Casey Winthrop tells me."

Father Carmody declined Phil's invitation to stay on to watch a televised game. Notre Dame was playing a formidable Big East opponent.

"I think I jinx them when I watch."

"Where did you park?"

"Park? I walked."

No wonder he had arrived half frozen. Phil said he would drive the priest back to Holy Cross House. Father Carmody did not argue. Alone, Roger sat in the specially constructed desk chair in his study, moving now left, now right, a compromised compass, thinking. The most obvious suspect in any attack on David Williams would be Timothy Quinn, but what would he be doing in Kentucky?

Amanda called to report that Jay's roommate had said that he had left campus, anticipating the Thanksgiving break.

"Where?"

"He and his father plan to celebrate together."

PART THREE

REQUIEM

1 ➤ AS SOON AS THE WHITE BUILDINGS
of the monastery came into view, the Knight
brothers felt enveloped in rural peacefulness. Phil had almost
missed the turnoff to Bardstown, and for twenty minutes there had
been silence in the van, as if both brothers were wondering if they
were lost. Then the sight of the monastery dissolved their doubt.

"I told you I'd find the place," Phil said, but there was relief in
his voice.

"I never doubted you."

"I'll report you to Descartes."

Worse than the doubt had been the discomfort of the unbroken
trip from South Bend. Roger's swivel chair in the back of the van
gave him the appearance of a turret gunner, a very well fed turret
gunner, but even this special seat seemed inadequate. He must
have gained weight. "Or the chair has shrunk." With Phil's help,
Roger had squeezed in. The safety belt didn't have enough give to
encircle Roger, so Phil had disengaged the signal that otherwise
would have scolded them throughout the trip. Phil had suggested a
rest stop several times, but Roger didn't dare get out of the seat, so
it was with some discomfort that he arrived.

Getting out of the van was the first order of business, made even
more difficult by the fact that the circulation in Roger's legs had

been cut off during the long cramped ride. After several unsuccessful efforts to free him, Phil sought and found help.

"He only weighed one hundred twenty pounds when we set out," Phil told the two monks who answered his summons. "I don't know what happened to him."

"Puffed up with pride." His feet on the ground, Roger rose slowly, then fell back against the van. "My legs are numb."

Walking was the proposed remedy, and soon Roger was being helped along the walk to the guesthouse, leaning on two thin monks, a wounded athlete being taken from the field.

Chadwick had signed them up as retreatants, but they would be on their own unless they asked for spiritual direction. The task they had come on would be better performed without fanfare. The guest master, of indeterminate age, crew-cut hair, spare of body beneath the white habit, took one look at Roger and said he would give him a room on the first floor of the guesthouse.

The single room was narrow, chalk white walls, unadorned except for a crucifix. On a bedside table was an alarm clock. One straight-back chair.

"Wonderful," Roger said. "As in causing wonder."

The serenity of the monk's smile was reminder enough that he was not engaged in banter with Emil Chadwick. The monk gave him directions to the bathroom, and Roger immediately set off for it.

They were on their own. No schedule other than what they devised for themselves, although of course they were welcome to come to chapel during the chanting of hours and the community Mass. Roger asked the guest master if he would let Brother Chrysologus know they were here. Emil had confided in his son that the brothers were coming down on behalf of the university.

Now that he was on his feet again and his legs obeyed his commands, Roger wandered outside and marveled at the silence, of the house and of the world around the monastery. They were scarcely an hour from modern normalcy, and yet Roger felt that he had been dropped into an earlier time. The few signs that this was indeed the twenty-first century and not the fifth or twelfth were easily ignored, and this gave a powerful sense of the role monasticism had played in the formation of Europe and throughout the ages of faith until the apostles of reason had systematically shut down religious houses in the name of progress. Now, after bloody revolutions and bloodier wars following on the elegant naïveté of the Enlightenment, monasticism was making a comeback.

In the United States, the revival had started after World War II when the gifted Thomas Merton, who had come to Gethsemani to take the vows of a Trappist, published his autobiography, *Seven Storey Mountain*. His further writings had acquainted his generation with the possibility of a monastic vocation, and Trappist abbeys had spread across the land. It is the fate of every male visitor to a monastery to imagine himself as a part of the community, living a scheduled day, work and prayer, work and prayer, a life of quiet and obedience seemingly without a worry in the world. Romantic, of course, yet Roger momentarily entered into the fantasy. But it was too self-regarding. Men did not become monks in order to please themselves, although if one were called to it such a life must have its profound satisfactions. The stripping away of distractions was meant to remove impediments to the acquisition of holiness. Monks saw their lives as a service to the Church, to the world, much as Benedict all those centuries ago had fled Rome and become first a hermit and then founded the community at Subiaco. Eventually that community ended at Monte Cassino, the great monastery that had been bombarded during World War II, becoming briefly a battleground as the Allies moved slowly up the Italian peninsula.

The fantasy wore off as Roger walked and surveyed the fields and woods of the vast monastery grounds. He would have to settle for these few days, in which he could review the state of his soul. And talk with Brother Joachim.

And find out who had killed Dave Williams.

Brother Chrysologus and Phil were chatting in an open area of the guesthouse when Roger returned. The monk rose to his feet when Phil introduced his brother. For all his spiritual discipline, he could not disguise his reaction to Roger's massive presence.

"Are all the monks as thin as you, Brother?"

"We have one or two chubby ones."

"Chubby wouldn't do to describe me. I wonder if I could see Brother Joachim."

"I will get word to him."

"He doesn't know me. Tell him I have come from Notre Dame."

Chrysologus nodded, and Roger left the two to their conversation, collapsing in a chair across the room.

"Professor Knight?"

A startled Roger swam out of the sleep into which he had sunk moments after sitting down.

The monk standing beside his chair smiled apologetically. "I'm Brother Joachim. You wanted to see me?"

"Yes, I do. Yes. Please sit down. That will be easier than my standing up."

Joachim was over six feet tall but looked taller because of his slenderness. His hands were in the sleeves of his white habit, crossed over the black scapular. His face was thin and his pouched eyes large and deep. He took a seat next to Roger's. "You're from Notre Dame."

"Yes, yes, I am."

"I went to Notre Dame."

"I know. Class of '89. I have seen the materials you sent to the archives."

A nod. "Now you have come to investigate the death of David Williams."

"Brother Chrysologus has offered to show us the hermitage."

The abbey had a vehicle about the size of a golf cart for getting around the grounds, and it was put at their disposal. Chrysologus declined Phil's offer of the passenger seat and walked beside them as they went out to the hermitage. The trees here were not as far along to winter as those in Indiana, but already the ground around them was carpeted with fallen leaves, their colors fading.

"This is the way you took with Casey Winthrop?" Roger asked Chrysologus.

A nod of his crew-cut head. "Of course, we were both walking."

Not a criticism, apparently. With monks you had to fight the impulse to ask what had brought them to this secluded demanding life. Roger had read that clients often quizzed fallen women in much the same way.

Emil Chadwick had been unable to explain it when Roger asked him about his son's vocation to the Trappists. "He was as nutty as any other kid. Not much of a student, I'm afraid. Except for Latin. He loved Latin. Sometimes I had the idea that he was observing things and people in disbelief. 'Is this all there is?' Not criticizing, you understand. Just a little baffled. He translated Horace's *Ars Poetica* for his senior essay. He loved Horace. So did Kant." Emil added enigmatically. "The preface to the *Kritik*."

Emil was full of arcane lore, which was why Roger had been drawn to him from the time he first moved into the office in Brownson. Emil had surveyed Roger's girth and said, "Welcome to Fat City."

Sarah, who was there at the time, took umbrage.

"My dear, you are sylphlike."

"What's a sylph?"

"Look it up," Emil said with a teacher's reflex.

"Is it naughty?"

"Not always."

Roger had called Emil to tell him that he and Phil were going to Gethsemani.

"How?"

"Phil's driving."

"Tell him not to get lost."

"He has a GPS."

"What in hell is that?"

Emil had lived through the transition from mechanical typewriters to computers, from wired phones to cell phones, from reasonably educated entering students to the illiterate youth of his last years of teaching—his description—but then they knew all sorts of things that were mysteries to him.

When the hermitage came in sight, Roger brought the vehicle to a stop and Phil hopped out.

"Leave it here, Roger."

Phil and Chrysologus were halfway to the hermitage before Roger had his feet on the ground. He lumbered after them. Chrysologus had stopped to tell Phil that it was just about here that he had whistled to let Joachim know of their approach. Joachim had then appeared, coming out of the woods behind the little building. Onto the porch then. Chrysologus took Roger's hand and helped him up the steps. Phil wanted a description of that earlier arrival. The monk had to think to get the sequence right. Had he tried to open the inner door before Joachim joined him and Casey? Roger was looking at the neatly stacked firewood on the porch of the hermitage, just beside the door. He picked up a piece as they went inside.

There was a flagstone fireplace in the front room, the only heating in the place. Two more or less comfortable chairs angled toward the fireplace. A statue of Our Lady on the mantel, next to the crucifix. It was tempting to take one of those chairs, to just sit there and use the place for the purpose it was intended. Solitude. Silence. Meditation. On the wall was a framed photograph of Jacques Maritain and Thomas Merton seated before this very fireplace. Phil tried the door that separated this room from those beyond, moving it on its hinges.

"He was lying there," Chrysologus said, pointing.

"Feet first, head first?"

The monk closed his eyes, as if to evoke the scene. "He had fallen with his head toward the front of the hermitage."

"Facedown?"

"Facedown."

The murder weapon, a piece of firewood, still lay where the assailant had dropped it.

Phil was drawn to the back door at the end of the hallway separating the oratory from the bedroom and bathroom. He tried it. Unlocked.

"Was this door open or shut?"

Roger could see what Phil was getting at, but there was a difficulty. Someone—Joachim?—had come in through that back door and struck David Williams from behind, which was why he fell forward, toward the front of the building.

"The firewood is on the front porch, Phil."

"There's more out back," Chrysologus said.

More indeed. It was stacked four or five feet high along the back wall of the building. In the little clearing beyond was a huge stump surrounded with chips. An axe wrapped in plastic lay atop the stacked firewood.

"Chopping wood for the fireplace is the main exercise you have here. That and walking."

"Have you ever stayed here?"

"No."

"Don't you take turns using it?"

"Only if you ask permission."

Phil went outside, to scout around, Chrysologus with him. Roger stood in the doorway of the bedroom, looking around. Bare as a cell, which is what it was. The bed was so narrow that he would have spilled over its sides, if indeed it could support his weight. Steel frame, no headboard, a thin-looking mattress with a comforter drawn over it. Did monks still sleep in their habits?

Roger returned to the front room and eased himself into one of the chairs. Phil had wanted to inspect the hermitage before they talked with Joachim. The grate of the fireplace was clean, no ashes, no sign of a recent fire. The nights here must already be cold, but then that provided an occasion for asceticism. Roger closed his eyes, trying to imagine what had happened here.

Joachim and Dave Williams would have sat in these very chairs, talking of their time at Notre Dame. It could hardly have been simply nostalgia. Over the years, Joachim had sent cards to Dave that could be regarded as menacing. Then had come the donation to the archives, an equivocal short story, and the huge bequest to Dave. And reference to a murder that had not been committed! Yes, theirs must have been an interesting conversation.

The monk then had excused himself and gone out for a walk during which he said his rosary. Apparently he had heard nothing, had no inkling that they had been joined by an intruding third party. From the description of the body, David Williams could have been returning from the bathroom. Or using the oratory, of course, though that seemed less likely. Nature before grace. The assailant could have been waiting on the back porch, able to see inside through the little window in the door, and, when David emerged from the bathroom, rushed in and felled him. Roger could almost see the scene. But who had been holding that piece of firewood?

Of course, the obvious suspect was Joachim, the monk who had been sending David Williams veiled, almost threatening, messages over the years, the classmate who had sent those materials to the Notre Dame archives with the absurd confessional letter and the bequest of all his worldly goods to David Williams. They must indeed have had an interesting conversation there before the fireplace. Surely Joachim would have dropped the oblique approach and told David of the stillborn infant he had helped Beth bury near the Log Chapel. How would Dave have reacted to that? In fact, what would have been the point of telling him after all these years? Had an old grudge been nursed all this time, despite the years in the monastery? It was clear to Roger that Phil leaned toward Joachim.

"Phil, he's a monk."

"Wasn't Rasputin a monk?"

2) JOACHIM'S ACCOUNT OF THAT LONG-
ago burial near the Log Chapel on campus
was undramatic. Terse. Trimmed of all incidentals. He and Roger
had gone outside and sat in a courtyard in whose center a fountain
sent up an endless spout of water.

When the then Pat Pelligrino had been confronted by the tragic
figure of Beth, clutching to her bosom something wrapped in a bath
towel, and asked what was the matter, she had turned back a corner
of the towel and showed him.

"She was like the Pietà. She wanted to know what to do. It was I
who suggested the burial." He ran a finger down the long line of his
nose. "It has plagued my conscience ever since."

"Surely you don't think it was wrong."

A taste of Trappist silence. "I don't think it was right."

More silence, and then he went on. "I wanted to kill Dave."

"Beth told you he was the father?"

"She didn't have to. It certainly wasn't me, and Tim Quinn's reaction told me it wasn't him."

"Leaving Dave Williams?"

"Tim wanted to kill him. So did I. I really did. It was jealousy we
felt, of course."

"What was Dave's reaction?"

Joachim turned to Roger. "After Tim disappeared, my anger left me. I felt it was up to Beth to tell him if anyone did."

"And she didn't."

"Apparently not. Terrible as all that was, it changed our lives. Beth with her homeless center. That stillborn child was a turning point in her life. Things could never be the same again for her. She didn't want them to be. She was beyond all of us now. She had outlived us. How shallow and facetious we must have looked to her after what she had gone through. Eventually we were all affected, directly or indirectly. Tim's disappearance was a first result, and now we find that he had become like one of those wandering holy men in Tolstoy."

"And you in a Trappist abbey?"

"You can leave the world, but it never really leaves you."

"I suppose Dave wanted to thank you for giving him all that money."

"I was more concerned with the state of his soul. It seemed wrong that the father shouldn't know."

"What would be the point of that now?"

"Imagine first encountering the soul of an unknown daughter in paradise."

"So you sent him annual cards."

"I hoped he would come see me."

"Finally he did."

"God rest his soul."

"Amen. Have you heard from Quinn since his reappearance?"

"Oh, he was here."

"He was?"

"Just the other day. He said he'd be back."

———

After he left Joachim, Roger talked to the guest master, who seemed surprised that Roger wanted to check his register of guests. When he understood the role the Knight brothers were playing, he was delighted. He leaned toward Roger and whispered, "I've read all of Agatha Christie. Twice."

It was surprising to find that John Donne had spent two nights in the guesthouse. Quinn? Lawrence Briggs had also been there.

"How long did Briggs stay?"

"Just the one night, apparently. He left without telling me. Of course, there was a great deal of commotion when they brought Dave Williams to the infirmary."

The guest master talked of Briggs while Roger continued to look at the registry. There was no entry for Jay Williams.

Phil put through a call to Father Carmody, to let him know that recent events in Kentucky posed no threat to Notre Dame's reputation. Roger wandered outside and got into the little battery-powered vehicle that was at his disposal and moved out silently along the road. The vehicle itself was a Trappist of sorts, hardly a purr out of it. Its speed was conducive to thought.

He drove to within six feet of the steps leading to the front porch of the hermitage. What spiritual dramas had been enacted here? He recalled the photograph of Merton and Maritain on the wall inside. There are sacred spaces, churches, hermitages. Log chapels. A murder in such a place was akin to sacrilege.

"There was a Notre Dame student down here at the time," Phil said.

"Who?"

"The guest master didn't register him. He was just here for the day, apparently."

Jay Williams? He had left campus . . .

"Father Carmody wants Williams's body brought back to Notre Dame for burial."

"I wonder if Jay Williams would agree to that."

"He already has. Carmody asked him when he gave him the sad news. But only if his mother could be reburied there."

When they returned, Phil took the stick of firewood with him, along with a plaster cast of some shoe prints at the back entrance to the hermitage. Street shoes. Not the shoes of a monk.

3 A GARBLED VERSION OF WHAT HAD
happened in the hermitage at Gethsemani
Abbey had reached the Old Bastards and was Topic A at their table
in Leahy's.

"Emil Chadwick's son is a monk there," Armitage Shanks reminded them.

"Are you accusing him?"

Potts was indignant. "Emil wouldn't hurt a fly."

"Tell it to Spider-Man."

"Spider-Man?" Bingham had surprised them all.

"Did you ever hear the story of the man who went to Lourdes and got sick?"

Horvath threw up his hands. "Father Sorin would have attacked you with a piece of firewood if he heard you say such a thing."

The devotion of the founder of Notre Dame to Our Lady of Lourdes was well known. The Grotto on campus, a replica of the original in the little town in the Pyrenees, attested to that.

"Did you ever go there, Horvath?"

"Lourdes? Not yet."

The thought of the hobbling Horvath boarding a plane to fly off to the distant shrine filled them all with glee.

Armitage Shanks rapped the table for order. "The question is, what will happen next in this unfolding saga of selected members of the class of 1989?"

"Isn't David Williams the man who promised twenty million dollars to Notre Dame?"

"He is."

"For a new ethics center. We have discussed this."

"But since then he has been murdered in a monastery while visiting his classmate the monk."

"There is a connection?"

"Everything is connected," Potts proclaimed.

"Except your hearing aid."

Called to replenish their drinks, Murph the bartender asked if they had heard the latest. Six attentive pairs of eyes lifted to him.

"The bar and restaurant will be open on Thanksgiving."

"On a holy day?"

"Murph, you should spend that day in the bosom of your family. You do have one?"

"Bosom?"

"Get out of here."

"They're hiring a substitute for the day."

"Murph, there is no substitute for you," Armitage said unctuously.

"There's scarcely an original."

"Will your substitute be male or female?"

"They won't know until after the operation."

"Keep it up, Murph, and we'll make you an honorary Old Bastard."

"I'm overwhelmed." He went back to his bar.

"Why is no one simply whelmed?" Horvath asked.

Bingham asked for attention. "The Knight brothers went off to the monastery. On behalf of the university."

"Who are the Knight brothers?"

"Doris Day's cousins."

"Doris Day!" The old faces lit up with memories of the lilting songs of that lovely chanteuse. Of course Bingham had to spoil it.

"Oscar Levant said he had known her *before* she was a virgin."

The groans and hissing drew the attention of other patrons. Then their drinks arrived and the noise subsided. The groans began again when Bingham said that if he had become a monk he would have taken for his name in religion Brother Darwin.

4 WHEN BETH GOT THE NEWS OF THE
death of Dave Williams in the Trappist mon-
astery in Kentucky from Casey, she left her office and went upstairs
to her studio. A gray sky was visible through the skylight, matching
her mood. The man by whom she had become pregnant was dead,
the father of her stillborn infant. Had Joachim told him the full
story?

Beth resolved to have a Mass said for Dave Williams. After a
period during which it had been hoped that Dave might recover, he
had succumbed to a clot in the brain. At first Beth had thought what
a blessing it was to leave the world in such surroundings, but Dave
had left it for all practical purposes when he had been hit over the
head.

"He had a priest?"

"He was surrounded by priests. Even his doctor was a priest.
Brother Bernard."

Beth took consolation from that. A monk who was a doctor would
know when his role as priest should come into play.

Casey seemed almost sheepish about telling her that he was a
father of a bouncing boy. Peaches was doing well.

"Peaches?"

"My wife. Patricia. They always called her Peaches. She wants to
name our son David." He didn't sound excited by the idea.

"Did she know him?"

"Oh, sure. He had a place down here, he and Bridget."

"Bridget?"

"His late wife."

"Were there children?"

"One son. At Notre Dame."

How little she knew of those long-lost friends, suddenly found again because Pat Pelligrino had stirred things up with his gift to the Notre Dame archives.

"You'll tell Quinn, won't you?"

"He's not here at the moment."

"Not back yet? He came to see me."

"In Florida?"

"Just passing through. He didn't stick around long enough to meet Peaches."

"Did he say where he was going?"

"Back there eventually. Via Gethsemani."

The portrait she had been doing was missing from her easel when she got back from Notre Dame. Beth shook her head. Could anyone sustain hatred for decades? Apparently Tim could. Well, say it, she still felt for Dave what she had felt long ago.

After hanging up, Beth looked around to see who could look after things while she ran up to Holy Rosary. If only Q were around when she needed him. Had Houdini ever made himself disappear? It seemed to be Q's only trick.

"Me?" asked Foster when she spoke to him. Bald as an egg, roly-poly, hardly over five feet high, he was a contrast to the withered physiques of the other guests. Foster had taken over in the kitchen when Q was nowhere to be found. A secret drinker, he stashed his bottle among the foodstuffs in the cupboards. The cheapest of wines, bought with the proceeds from his daily panhandling. He claimed to be on the wagon, of course. Beth had become patient with drinkers, for the most part. There was often the beginning of true humility in their inability to master alcohol. Knowing they were unable to control their longing for drink, hating the habit, they were open to the only real help there is.

"You can do it," she told Foster.

"How long will you be gone?"

"An hour at most."

Foster looked around, as if wondering what he would do should there be an uprising among the guests. It was midafternoon, a dead time. The television was on, ignored by dozing guests. Many were over in the residence, napping, sleeping it off, any kind of unconsciousness in a pinch. Our Lady of the Road left rehabilitation to others, accepting the present condition of the men who wandered in, not preaching to them, but hoping they would find in the depths to which they had sunk a saving sign of being a creature.

Foster was rummaging in the kitchen cupboard when she went out the door.

Father Romanus did not express surprise when Beth showed up at the rectory, although this was not the usual day for their weekly talk. He was the third Dominican from whom she had sought direction—first Justin, then Reynolds, red haired, his habit big as a tent, baby faced, and the wisest of them all. His name in religion was Thomas Aquinas. Romanus was solid, incapable of surprise, full of knowledge of Teresa of Ávila. Beth hadn't hit if off with St. Catherine of Siena, but Teresa of Ávila never failed her.

"I want to have a Mass said. For the father of my child."

He had taken her into one of the rectory parlors, furnished in basic Dominican, and didn't ask her what that meant. Years ago Beth had joined what was then called the Third Order of St. Dominic, but Justin had told her she needn't come to the meetings. Once had been enough. How good the others were, how uneventful their lives. Ordinary people. Is there any other kind? Well, there was the kind who came as guests to Our Lady of the Road. At the meeting someone had grumped about catering to all the drunks in the area. "Feed them and there will be more."

"Let's hope so," Beth had said.

That guy would have been the ruin of her. How superior she had felt answering him, as if she were a model of anything. So she had become a freelance lay Dominican, her weekly conferences her lifeline. At the same meeting a woman had gushed over the fact that when they died they could be buried in the Dominican habit.

"Why wait?"

Oh, she had been terrible. Father Justin had agreed. She had all she could handle at Our Lady of the Road. Any temptation to smugness there was quickly knocked out of her.

Justin had approved of her observing the birthday of her miscarried child. "Ask her to pray for you."

It wasn't until Justin was replaced by Thomas Aquinas Reynolds that Beth had someone willing to talk about the condition of the departed souls. He was full of lore from Aquinas, the *Summa*, other works, commentaries on Scripture.

"How can they remember us if they lack the physical presuppositions of memory, you ask? Call it the brain. That's dust now. But we pray to the saints, for particular favors. If they had no memory of the world we're in they wouldn't get it at all."

Those sessions had been almost fun, but the priest was not into idle speculation. His firm guide was Scripture, what the Church taught, and no wild guessing about or imagining the next world. "It is a holy and wholesome thought to pray for the dead." And it was a two-way street.

Beth had baptized her baby and named her Mary.

Romanus knew her story. Each of her advisers had; how else could they understand why she lived the way she did? The priest had uncapped a fat old-fashioned fountain pen and drawn a little pad toward him. "Name?"

He meant David's. She told him; his pen scratched on the pad. He actually blotted it. When had she last seen that? She told him what she knew of David's death, that he had died in a Trappist abbey.

"So did St. Thomas Aquinas. When's the funeral?"

"Father, I don't see how I can go. I'm sure it will be at Notre Dame."

"What's the problem?"

She explained about Q's absence and described Foster.

"He often drops by."

"Foster?"

"For a handout. Look, Beth, go to the funeral. If it comes to that, I will look after things down there myself."

"Oh, would you?"

"Are you doubting my word?" But he smiled when he asked.

Walking back, she tried to feel more grateful than she was. She was almost reluctant to return to Notre Dame so soon after being there and coming away with the feeling that talking with Father Carmody, her alpha and omega, had put a fitting end to all that had happened. Still, of course she would go. How could she not? When she got back to Our Lady of the Road, she went up to her studio. The phone was ringing. It was Father Carmody.

5   JAY WILLIAMS WAS HAPPY TO LEAVE arrangements to Father Carmody, who had the body brought back to Notre Dame, made arrangements with Hickey the undertaker, and secured a plot in Cedar Grove Cemetery on what had been the sixteenth fairway when Dave Williams had played the course as a student. Then he made arrangements with Father Rocca, rector of Sacred Heart Basilica, for the funeral.

"You'll be saying the Mass, Father?" Father Rocca asked.

"Yes, Peter." He waited, tense, but that was all. He had been afraid the rector might volunteer to assist. He might have wanted to concelebrate.

"I'll be in the sanctuary."

"Thank God," he said fervently.

That done, he settled down to call the names on the little list he had made.

"Casey Winthrop called me, Father," Beth said when he got through to her. "Of course I'm coming."

"Bring Quinn."

"Father, he's disappeared."

"Not again!"

"Casey saw him in Florida."

"I hope Casey can come."

"He's just become a father."

Pray hold me excused? No, Casey said he had expected the call ever since leaving Gethsemani.

"I'll want to hear all about your visit there," Father Carmody told him. So would Phil Knight.

"What's to tell? I want my son baptized at Notre Dame."

"If you're asking me to do it, the answer is yes."

"Great."

He had had few chances for pastoral work over the years, a wedding now and again, lately funerals, hearing confessions in Sacred Heart. How long had it been since he had baptized a baby?

Father Carmody called the abbot to tell him that he hoped Father Joachim could come to the funeral. The abbot said it had been almost like losing one of his monks when David Williams died in the infirmary.

"He will be buried here, of course," Carmody said.

"Here?"

"At Notre Dame."

He was half afraid the abbot would suggest burying David Williams in with a bunch of monks. Of course, that was unlikely. How many nonmembers of the Congregation had been buried in their community cemetery? Not that there were a lot of requests.

"You want Joachim to say the Mass?" the abbot asked.

Father Carmody had not expected this, but what else would the abbot think? Otherwise attending the funeral might have seemed to him a mere pleasure trip. He shut his eyes and said, "We'll concelebrate."

It was beginning to look like a very small funeral. Would there be enough of David's old classmates to act as pallbearers? Next was Wheeling, current president of the class of 1989. He would spread the word.

Mame Childers reacted like Mame Childers. "Oh my God. Father, I had a premonition. I've often had them in the past. I knew it was too good to last. Nothing works out for me."

Well, grief is often self-referential.

"Has Jay been told, Father? His son?"

"You know him?"

"Of course I know him. We've become quite friends. It seemed the prudent thing to do."

Father Carmody forbore asking her how her monsignor was doing. Let her cherish the thought that she and David Williams would have married. The old priest had not had an opportunity to discuss Mame's letter from Monsignor Sparrow with Dave.

The reminder of the son diverted him to Roger Knight.

Phil answered. "He's sleeping, Father. He's all tuckered out."

"Sounds like a failed automobile."

A long pause. Phil would think he was getting as bad as Roger.

"Have him call me, will you, Phil?"

"Are you watching the game?"

"With the sound off." The picture, too. What game was Phil referring to? The man was such a sports nut it might have been lacrosse.

Father Carmody realized that he was enjoying being in charge, arranging things. Some of the old zest came back. He still had a few miles in him. Then he thought of the few miles that separated Holy

Cross House from the community cemetery. How long would it be before he was taken there from his own funeral Mass and interred with his brothers in religion, the strains of the *Salve Regina* sweetening the winter air? Winter? Make it summer. The summer after next. Or later. He went back to his list.

6 EMIL CHADWICK WAS DOZING OVER *The Devil's Dictionary* in his office in Brownson Hall; that is, the book was open on his lap, his eyes were closed, and he was aware of a familiar sound, the tolling of the bells of nearby Sacred Heart Basilica. He was almost as close to them as Quasimodo, but it was not only defective hearing that now made their sound more faint.

There had been a time in his life, say from around fifty to seventy-five, when the solemn tolling of those bells marked another entry in his personal necrology, another colleague gone, or another faculty spouse. Of course he had gone to such funeral Masses and as often as not on to the cemetery for the burial. The ultimate test of collegiality. He had buried friends and enemies alike. The bells no longer tolled for him. He was the sole survivor of those who had been on the faculty in his golden years. Unsurprisingly, given recent events, he remembered the tolling of those bells when there had been a memorial service for the supposedly late Timothy Quinn. Perhaps, like Huckleberry, young Quinn had taken some mordant pleasure, if only belated, in the thought of his own funeral. Chadwick stirred. There were times when he felt that his own funeral had already occurred. He opened his eyes and glanced at the book on his lap, only the top third of which was visible over the arc of his stomach.

FUNERAL, n.

A pageant whereby we attest our respect for the dead by enriching the undertaker, and strengthen our grief by an expenditure that deepens our groans and doubles our tears.

Not bad. Not terribly good either. Well, that was true of most of Ambrose Bierce's definitions. Once Chadwick had found that gloomy humor witty. Later, the entries came to seem forced. They were certainly uneven in quality.

Bierce had been raised in Indiana, just down the road from South Bend. Off to the Civil War, into journalism, to San Francisco, then Washington, and finally the mysterious disappearance in Mexico. There were precedents for Timothy Quinn. Actually, he was more like B. Traven than Bierce. Traven had survived his disappearance. Mexico again. What intrigued Chadwick was learning that Quinn had made his way back to the campus after discharge from the army and worked on the grounds crew.

"He said he operated a mower on the golf course," Roger Knight had said.

"Burke."

Roger didn't understand.

"The old golf course. Only half of it is left. I stopped golfing when they gobbled up the back nine for new buildings."

"You golfed?"

"Often, but not well. The risibly cheap season ticket was one of the few faculty perks in those days. In August, before they installed the sprinkling system, a topped ball could roll three hundred yards on the khaki fairways." Chadwick smiled into the past.

"He is an odd fellow, Emil."

Quinn. "Well, after all those years of being dead."

Roger had of course recounted to him his visit to Minneapolis to see Beth Hanrahan and the surprising discovery of Quinn as a volunteer in her center for wandering homeless souls. "He works in the kitchen. He makes the soup."

"Was he a cook in the army?"

"Just what I asked him. He said he wasn't that bad."

Chadwick smiled.

"I was in the navy, you know, Emil. The food wasn't bad at all. At any rate, I thrived on it. You might say that it contributed to my discharge."

Roger had a semidefensive habit of alluding to his enormous weight. He asked if Chadwick had read the stories in the student papers.

"Certainly not."

"There was going to be a revival of a play by Patrick Pelligrino. They intended to invite that group of students from the Class of 1989 to attend. The original cast. Of course, Brother Joachim could not have come."

"Meaning he wouldn't want to. Trappists can do such things nowadays. Don't forget that Joachim requested and was given permission to spend some time in the hermitage."

"The scene of the crime."

"It's where Thomas Merton hung out. To be alone. Merton didn't like community life."

Chadwick had visited the place with Maurice, Chrysologus, his son: a kind of camp, deep in the woods, a bedroom, an oratory, a kitchen, and a front porch where one had a wonderful view down a valley to some hills. He thought of his little house in Holy Cross Village. "We all end up monks of a sort."

"Beth Hanrahan has promised to come to the funeral."

"I would like to see her again."

"Again?"

"She came to me for directed readings." He laid his head on the back of his chair, thinking. "Hawthorne. We read Hawthorne." A long silence. "The thing that interested her most was the fact that Hawthorne's daughter became a Dominican nun."

Roger rose to go, asking if Emil would care for a cup of coffee.

"It would keep me awake."

The door closed. Now Emil turned the pages of his book.

CONVENT, n.

A place of retirement for women who wish for leisure to meditate upon the vice of idleness.

7 ROGER DID NOT HAVE MUCH TO SAY
when Phil ticked off the names of those he
considered suspects in the murder of David Williams. Phil expected a protest when he led off with Brother Joachim, but Roger just worked his lips in and out, breathing through his nose.

"Then there's Jay Williams."

"His son?"

Phil reminded him of what the guest master had said about the Notre Dame student who had visited Gethsemani on the day Williams was attack.

"That's pretty far-fetched, Phil. His own father?"

"It bears looking into. You're the one who told me what his girlfriend said."

Amanda Zikowski had indeed told Roger that she was worried about Jay. "He's afraid his father is going to get married again."

"That's not against the law, Amanda."

"You have to understand Jay's feeling for his mother. She's been gone years, yet he talks about her as if she's in the next room. He thinks it would be a betrayal."

"Have you made up with him?"

She smiled. "A cosmetic truce. He thinks because his father was a student actor it's in the genes."

Roger remembered that Jay had once asked him—seriously? as

part of his pranks?—if he could hire the Knight brothers to investigate his father. Concern with how the financial mess was affecting his father had been the reason given, but Amanda's remark made him wonder. If Jay had told Phil he wanted to know if his father had a girlfriend, he would have been out of luck. Phil never took divorce cases.

Phil had made a flying trip to New York and had not learned much. He had heard about Dave's liaison with Mame, but Father Carmody had assured him there was nothing to it.

Apparently, however, Jay had hired someone else. Phil had run into Ziggy Cobalt in Leahy's. Ziggy was a private eye, his preferred self-description, and with lenses as thick as his, his eyes did seem to be enjoying their privacy.

"Knight!" Ziggy said, looking over both shoulders first.

"What brings you here?"

Ziggy winked in reply. "Now, now, you know that's not an appropriate question."

Later Phil asked Murph if Ziggy had talked with him.

"He's talked with everybody. He says he's a private eye."

"Then he must be out on parole."

"You know him?"

"I did. Before his conviction. What's he looking for?"

"You got me."

"He's been in prison?"

"I'm kidding. Ziggy has no convictions."

Phil had tailed Ziggy to the residence in which Jay Williams lived. Had Ziggy told Jay about Mame? Father Carmody might dismiss it, but Phil thought otherwise.

Phil went on with his list. "Then there is Timothy Quinn."

Roger rotated his wheeled chair. "That would seem more likely, but you would have to place him at the monastery at the time." He thought of the name John Donne entered in the guesthouse registry and of Joachim's remark.

Phil didn't think a lot of the list himself, but what else did he have? The biggest problem was jurisdiction—if there was even a charge. There was a sheriff in the county in which Gethsemani was located, a man named Casper, whom Phil had looked up before they headed back to Notre Dame. Casper was what Roger would call taciturn. When he did speak it was emphatically.

"I don't want to tangle with those monks."

"Someone has been murdered, Sheriff."

"Is that right? No one ever told me about it. Where you from, son?"

Casper might have been a month or two older than Phil. Was this a sense of turf, or an exaggerated respect for the separation of church and state?

"I work out of New York. I'm living at Notre Dame now."

"Notre Dame!"

"It's a university in Indiana."

"I know what it is. LSU cleaned their clock last year." Casper's narrow eyes grew narrower. "You working for those monks?"

Phil gave up. Apparently the abbot had seen no need to call the sheriff because David Williams had died in the monastery infirmary. Wise as a serpent or simple as a dove? Maybe Casper wouldn't have taken his call. If he ever did find out who had dealt the ultimately mortal blow to David Williams, Phil wondered, where would he go with the information?

Roger said, "Well, Phil, they should all be here for the funeral."

"Is Quinn coming?"

"No one can find him to tell him what has happened."

Father Carmody was obviously of two minds. Phil sat with him in his room, watching vagrant snowflakes float by the window. Winter was on its way, and when winter came to Indiana it was, as Roger said, unequivocal winter. Father Carmody had enlisted Phil's help to find out what had happened to David Williams in the hermitage at Gethsemani, so of course all he had to do was fire him if he wanted to. There had been little publicity about the murder, indeed no charge of murder, and Father Carmody liked that fine. The less danger of a blemish on the reputation of Notre Dame, the better. Who knew what Phil might turn up that would reflect adversely on Notre Dame? Or give her enemies cause for gossip?

"There's no doubt that his death was due to that blow on the head?" Father Carmody asked this as he expelled cigarette smoke. He might have wanted to see what it would sound like if spoken aloud. Phil said nothing to this, but when he described his conversation with Sheriff Casper, the old priest's integrity was put to a real test.

"There's no official acknowledgment of murder?"

"Casper knows nothing about it."

"So what are we investigating?"

"The murder of David Williams."

Phil could see how much Carmody would like to say, *Let sleeping dogs lie. Let Dave Williams rest in peace. If the sheriff down there doesn't care, why should we?* Care legally, that is. Of course he couldn't bring himself to say that.

There had been an autopsy when the body arrived in South Bend, but the blow on the head from which Dave had died might have been caused by an accident. The wound was included in the autopsy and the body turned over to Hickey.

"Maybe you'll never find out who did it, Phil."

"That's more than possible."

This cheered Carmody up. It made Phil all the more eager to find who had brought that chunk of firewood down on David Williams's head. Even if Carmody had told him to forget it, he would have gone on with the investigation.

8 BROTHER CHRYSOLOGUS WROTE TO his father to say that the abbot was sending him to Notre Dame as companion to Joachim for the funeral of David Williams, making it sound like a matter of obedience, as doubtless it was. Emil Chadwick did not often hear from his Trappist son, which, he supposed, was as it should be. When you leave the world you should cut your lines to it. To be sure, there was a filial letter at Christmas and from time to time a postcard—birthday wishes or the anniversary of his mother's death—but Maurice had entered the monastery and meant to give it all he had.

Emil Chadwick, on his rare visits—his coming to Gethsemani was all right since presumably it had a religious as well as paternal motive—had pieced together his son's attitude toward the life he led. There was no doubt that he was a Cistercian of the Strict Observance, the official title of the Trappists. In his letter, he alluded to the attack on David Williams, regretting that it had occurred on sacred soil as much as that it was a murder, and added, "Perhaps we should tear down the place." He meant the hermitage.

There is an old quarrel between monks concerning the relative merits of the hermetic life and community life. Thomas Merton had actually argued that the hermetic was the original Trappist charism. For Maurice, unlike for hundreds of others, Thomas Merton had been an obstacle rather than a spur to his vocation. Before entering, he had read Mott's life of Merton and Furlong's earlier one and been disenchanted. The hermitage had been built at Merton's request, and the author had spent much time out there in the woods, endlessly writing, sipping wine, listening to Joan Baez records, becoming more and more political, fascinated by Eastern religions. The hermitage had become a place where he could entertain friends and fans far from the eye of the abbot. After he had entered, Maurice never said such things; he didn't have to. While strict silence and its accompanying sign language were things of the past with Trappists, there is, after all, body language. Chrysologus made it clear enough to his father that the identification of Gethsemani with Thomas Merton displeased him.

Getting to Sacred Heart for the funeral posed a slight problem. It was one thing for Chadwick to pedal to his office on his three-wheeled cycle, but rolling up to the basilica in it would cause an unwelcome stir.

"I'll come for you," Roger Knight said. "We'll go together."

A golf cart wasn't much of an improvement over his tricycle, but Emil accepted gladly. Roger struck him as a bright light in otherwise dark days for the university and an ideal companion at funerals.

Roger made his offer in Brownson when Chadwick showed him the letter from his son.

"I can count the times I have seen him say Mass. I mean alone. At the monastery they say it together with the abbot."

There was a thump on the door of Chadwick's office, in which he and Roger were talking. Another thump, the door swung open, and a radiant Sarah, now large with child, stood there.

"I got it!" she cried.

Sarah had been offered the tenured professorship.

"Will you accept?"

She stared at him, shocked, until she saw that he was being facetious.

"Congratulations," Roger said, taking her hand. She threw herself into his arms and kissed his cheek. "Now, now."

At his desk, Chadwick strained forward, offering his own cheek. He got his kiss, and the elated Sarah seemed to float out of the room.

"Ah, youth," sighed Chadwick.

That was on a Tuesday. The funeral would be the following day. Father Carmody had decided that a viewing of the body would be held in the Lady Chapel of the basilica for an hour before the funeral Mass.

9 ⟶ PLANES, TRAINS, AND BUSES ARRIVE
at the South Bend airport, but Beth Hanrahan stayed on the limo she had taken from Chicago, having come there from Minneapolis by train. The so-called limo, actually a bus, after a first stop at the airport, continued to the Notre Dame campus, and it was at the bus stop there that Roger met her in his golf cart. She was wearing a purple beret and a black coat that seemed too large for her and was carrying a sport bag. Her eyes expressed pleasure at the sight of Roger, who had pushed back the hood of his parka as if she would have trouble recognizing him.

"I don't know where I'm staying," she said, hopping in.

"It's all been arranged."

"Don't tell me it's a motel."

The residence in which the trinity had lived was now a women's dorm, and the nun in charge was delighted at the prospect of putting Beth up there in a guest room. "Beth Hanrahan," she said breathily. "What an inspiration she is. Perhaps she'll give a talk at the Center for Social Concerns."

Beth's eyes widened when he told her this. Apparently a group of students had been brought to Our Lady of the Road to impress upon them their obligation to help the needy.

"A kind of slumming. Oh, I shouldn't say that. They seem to think my life is romantic."

"Any word from Timothy Quinn?"

She looked at him, then shook her head.

It had been trying to snow for days, without success, and the campus had the bleak look of late autumn, the trees stripped of their leaves, which had been gathered by the grounds crew and spirited away, the grass dull and brittle looking. Students moved along the walks, all bundled up, chattering into their cell phones, elsewhere no matter where they were.

"Have you eaten?"

"I packed a lunch."

"But you've been traveling all day. We'll get you settled, and then you'll come home with me. I'll make spaghetti."

"Oh, you mustn't go to any bother."

She acquiesced when she understood that she would be sharing Roger's and Phil's supper.

"Father Carmody will join us."

"Oh, good."

A delegation waited on the steps of the residence hall, and Beth was led triumphantly inside. The nun was not pleased that Roger intended to take away this honored guest almost immediately. Beth pleaded that she would be dining with Father Carmody.

"It's all arranged," Roger said.

Father Carmody was napping in his room when Roger called to invite him for a spaghetti dinner that night. Having accepted, the old priest rolled over and tried to get back to sleep. He was bushed, no doubt about it, but there was a glow of satisfaction as well. He was almost looking forward to David Williams's funeral.

Peter Rocca would pick up Brothers Chrysologus and Joachim

when they flew in. The monks would be lodged in Corby Hall, where many of the priests lived. A couple of Trappists in their midst ought to brighten up the place. He was smiling when he drifted back into dreamland.

Philip Knight came to Holy Cross House for him, a courtesy Father Carmody would usually argue about before accepting. Phil drove with the enthusiasm of a NASCAR fan, making conversation difficult. It was just as well. Father Carmody wasn't sure that he liked Phil calling the funeral a gathering of the suspects.

Phil had an odd request. "Remember being told that Timothy Quinn came back here during his lost years and worked for a time on the grounds crew?"

"Strange fellow."

"I wonder if he's strange enough to do it again."

Father Carmody thought about it. "I can find out."

"I was hoping you would."

"Anytime you want a partner on a wild goose chase, I'm your man."

Roger, wrapped in a massive apron, let them into the apartment, which seemed filled with steam. Beth Hanrahan came forward to greet the priest. She told him where she was staying.

"Good Lord."

He settled into what Roger called "his" chair and took the glass Phil handed him, brought it under his nose, and inhaled. "Happy days." He paused, aware of the inappropriateness of his toast. "You know what I mean."

Phil lifted his drink, and Roger and Beth toasted with their lemonade.

"I suppose you have to be a teetotaler," Carmody growled to Beth.

"Living among alcoholics is a sobering experience."

"I could tell you some tales myself, but I don't want to shock you."

"Do you know any Dominicans, Father?"

Carmody shifted in his chair. "A few."

"Dogs of the Lord," Roger said. *"Domini canes."*

In the ensuing silence, Father Carmody sipped his drink. "Why do you ask?"

"They've been very helpful to me in Minneapolis."

"They were the beatniks of their day when they began. Mendicants. A fancy name for panhandlers."

Beth laughed and told them about Foster, the cook who had replaced Timothy Quinn.

"Too bad Quinn won't be here. I'm short a pallbearer."

"I wonder if he would come if he knew."

"Why do you say that?"

Beth thought about it for a moment. "He made a great show of hating David's guts."

"Whatever for?" Carmody asked, then wanted to bite his tongue.

"It's easy to hate someone when you never see him," Beth said.

"It's easier when you do," the old priest said, then grinned at his own riposte.

There was red wine with the spaghetti and a huge platter of garlic bread. Roger had spread a checkered cloth, and the napkins were of the same material. Two candles glowed, prompting Carmody to tell a story of his seminary days, of how cold the chapel was in the morning, and the classmate who longed for a high Mass.

"Six candles then," he said. "Warmer." He looked around. "Not very funny. You'd be surprised what can amuse a seminarian."

After they had eaten, Beth helped Roger clean up, and Father Carmody went as if reluctantly into the television room with Phil.

"Did you ever watch Australian footfall, Father?"

"Only standing on my head."

"Of course, it's taped."

So were the players. They looked like the walking wounded of Gallipoli. What a brutal game.

Later, Beth managed to get him aside. "Father, I hope you won't think this is crazy, but I'll ask anyway."

He steeled himself for something odd, and it was odd. She wondered if he could possibly, while she was here, and given the occasion, bless the little grave by the back wall of the Log Chapel. He put a hand on her arm and nodded.

Mame was surprised when Wilfrid called to ask if she was going to Dave Williams's funeral. "How did you know he died?"

"It was in the *Times*."

Wilfrid wanted to come along.

"What on earth for?"

"I'm married to one of his clients."

For a change, Mame wasn't annoyed by this pretense that theirs was merely a temporary separation. Life with Wilfrid had been all right as long as he kept zipped up elsewhere. Well, who knows? The death of Dave Williams had cleared her emotional landscape. If there was a next time, she would call in Monsignor Sparrow. She felt she owed him that.

So they went to South Bend together. He got the loan of someone's plane, and they were whisked out in less than two hours. The plane would stay for them. Their rented car awaited them.

She had reserved a room at the Morris Inn, and there seemed no reason for Wilfrid to ask for another. Twin beds.

"It's the least I can do. You saved me plane fare."

He grinned like a boy.

"Don't get any ideas. Remember, we're here for a funeral."

Flying out, it had occurred to her that there was something weird about Wilfrid coming to Dave's funeral. He had hated Dave. He had tried to buy him off by opening an account with him. Mame solved the mystery by imagining that Will thought Dave's death cleared the way for their reunion. It looked like that was just what it was doing. Sometime during the night, she slipped into his bed, figuring they were as married now as they had ever been.

10 THE BELLS OF SACRED HEART WERE tolling mournfully as Beth Hanrahan made her way across campus from the residence hall in which she had spent the night. A light snow had fallen, leaving a soft blanket through which spears of grass emerged in a confusion of seasons. *VENITE AD ME OMNES,* read the legend on the statue of Jesus in front of the Main Building. A hearse was parked before the basilica, and other somber vehicles stood all in a row. A group of people clustered below the steps leading to the main entrance, the unmistakable figure of Roger Knight among them.

"Buon giorno," Roger said when she came up to him.

"Isn't that a pizza?" said the old man beside him, leaning on his walker.

"Emil, this is Beth Hanrahan."

"How you have changed, my dear." Then she remembered Professor Chadwick. She felt she was present at the general resurrection. She patted one of his hands that gripped the handle of the walker.

"I was afraid I would be late."

Professor Chadwick said, "Only one person need be late for a funeral."

"Hawthorne," Beth cried, suddenly remembering. She squeezed his hand.

"My scarlet letter gives me away."

Up the road, beyond the row of funereal vehicles, a large car arrived, the back doors were opened, and a man and woman emerged, she gorgeous in black, her face veiled. She hesitated before moving toward the basilica. When she did, the man followed like a bodyguard. She was about to go past their little group when she stopped.

"Beth!"

Beth felt frowsy indeed when addressed by this fashion plate. The veil was lifted.

"Mame?"

Mame flew at her and gathered her in her arms. Her escort remained discreetly in the background. He looked vaguely familiar to Beth.

"Your husband?"

"As was." When Mame stepped back, there were tears in her eyes. "Wilfrid. You were at our wedding."

"That's right."

"I can't believe that this has happened." She had turned to Roger. "What is being done to find out who did this?"

"Everything possible."

"I should hope so." She turned back to Beth. "Dave and I had become such friends of late." She dabbed at her unveiled eyes. The remark seemed freighted with meaning. Beth realized that Mame's getup almost suggested a mourning widow. "Is everyone here?"

No need to explain who everyone was.

"I don't see Timothy Quinn."

Above them, the mournful bells tolled on. The back door of the hearse was opened, revealing the casket. Silence fell. One of the undertaker's minions passed among them, suggesting that they go inside.

Mame said to Roger, in a whisper, "Is Jay here?"

He pointed. Jay Williams and three others were gathered around the open door of the hearse. Mame with a sigh identified him for Beth ("A dear boy"). Casey, looking uncomfortable in a suit, was there, too, and two others who turned out to be classmates Father Carmody had pressed into service as pallbearers. Peaches, all bundled up, held an equally bundled-up baby. All the women gathered around her.

Mame returned to Roger and said, "For heaven's sakes. What's he doing here?"

The man she indicated was off on the edge of the gathering.

"Who is he? "

"Larry Briggs." She made a face when she said it.

Roger was surprised. Briggs didn't look at all like the man the guest at the monastery master had described.

The others there at the entrance of the basilica comprised students, middle-aged couples, and a little band of ancient men, muttering among themselves. They might have been connoisseurs of funerals, lugubrious attendants at such events, as if they could not wait for their own. The undertaker was becoming insistent, and they went inside. Professor Chadwick was helped up the steps by Roger Knight, who needed help himself and got it from Beth. Inside, Professor Chadwick followed his walker up the aisle and they followed him.

"I cannot believe he's here," Mame said. Her flawless face had become a mask of fury.

Beth looked where Mame was looking and saw in a pew a tall stooped man, half turned toward them, who seemed intent on ignoring Mame. They moved slowly beyond him.

"Who is he?"

"Dave's nemesis. Larry Briggs." Mame almost hissed the words. "Why is he here?"

"Did he know Dave?"

"No!" After a pace or two, "Not in that sense. He was a client."

When they reached the front of the church, with reserved pews on each side, Professor Chadwick looked at Roger. "Bride or groom?"

Roger steered him into a pew on the left, and Beth, in the interests of balance, went with Mame and her husband into the second one on the right.

Mame sat, but when Beth knelt, she did, too. Wilfrid remained seated. The bells ceased tolling, and minutes later, from the sacristy, a procession emerged: priests, attendants, Father Carmody, beautifully vested, at the end. All rose. The procession went down a side aisle to the entrance where the casket now stood, and soon Father Carmody, after fussing with the microphone pinned to his chasuble, began to read from a book that an officious little fellow in cassock and surplice held before him. That done, a white cloth was draped over the casket, and Father Carmody led his fellow ministers up the aisle, the casket pushed after them by the pallbearers.

Another prayer from the steps of the sanctuary, and then Father Carmody moved to the presider's chair, where he was flanked by two tall ascetic priests with closely shaved heads. The little fellow in cassock and surplice stood by to smooth things, apparently the master of ceremonies, and another priest with a noble forehead, the rector of the basilica, wearing an alb, looked out over the congregation with dark expressive eyes. The familiar prayers of the Mass began. The first reading was done by a lovely young woman ("That must be Amanda," Mame whispered), the second by Roger Knight, who lumbered forward, climbed to the pulpit, and wedged himself in. Next, the gospel was read by Father Carmody, the story of the widow of Naim, and they all sat for the homily.

Father Carmody had not adopted the recent practice of canonizing the departed, depicting them as already enjoying heavenly bliss, but then he believed in purgatory. He spoke of Notre Dame and David Williams's formative years there and went on to speak of the fragility of life, and the inevitability of death, which comes like a thief in the night. ("Carrying a piece of firewood," Mame whispered.) They were all urged to draw profit from this salutary reminder of our common mortality, and that was pretty much it. From then on the Mass continued, interrupted now and then by the filling of the censer, which produced great clouds of smoke. Once Father Carmody came down and circled the casket, throwing up scented billows as he blessed it with the swinging censer.

"I had a late breakfast," Mame whispered when Beth rose to go up to receive communion.

Returned to her pew, kneeling, her face in her hands, Beth prayed to her sacramental Lord. Distracting thoughts came. Mame might be dressed for the role, but if anyone here was the ersatz widow, it was she herself. The sight of Dave's son, first outside the basilica, then kneeling in the pew before her, made her realize that he was the half brother of the daughter she would have had. For the first time she prayed fervently for her lover of so many years ago. The overwhelming sadness of things brought tears to her eyes, and she let them come. Where can you cry without exciting curiosity if not at a funeral? The irregular bond with Dave so many years ago, the link of that miscarried child buried in shame by the Log Chapel, their later lives, which, in Dave's case, had produced the fine young fellow in front of her—and now Dave was dead, murdered.

She wished she shared Mame's urgency that the culprit be found. She prayed for Q as well, wandering about, if not a lost soul, on his way to it.

Then it was over. They sang "Notre Dame, Our Mother"; they followed the casket back down the aisle.

"He's gone," Mame said. Apparently she meant the man named Briggs.

Outside, the casket was slid into the hearse, and Father Carmody and the two monks with him—Roger had told Beth who they were—got into a car to be driven to Cedar Grove Cemetery. Beth and Mame followed Roger's golf cart, Chadwick seated at his side, for the short walk to the cemetery.

"I loved him, Beth," Mame said, out of the blue. Wilfrid seemed not to have heard.

Beth found herself resenting Mame's widow's weeds and the proprietary air with which she spoke of David Williams. "We all did."

11 ⟶ DAVID WILLIAMS WAS TO BE BURIED
in the section of Cedar Grove Cemetery that
had been carved out of the former Burke Golf Course, a section
reached by a road angling around the sexton's shed. By the time the
walking mourners entered the cemetery, Mame was regretting that
they had sent the car back to the Morris Inn. Beth was unfazed by
the walking.

"What kind of shoes are those?" Mame asked her.

"I don't know."

"Where did you buy them?"

"Someone gave them to me." Immediately Beth regretted the remark. It sounded sanctimonious; maybe it was. It was difficult not to
be impressed by Mame's outfit, although those shoes were certainly
not made for walking.

"I wish I'd brought gym shoes," Mame said bravely.

Behind them, Casey, now carrying the baby, was walking with
Peaches. He had introduced her to everyone, proud as punch. Now
he was urging Jay to come visit them on Siesta Key. "Not in the
morning, though. I write in the morning." The planned talk had
been canceled as well as the play, giving way to the demands of fa-
therhood and Casey's writing schedule.

"I read *Tumbleweed*," Jay told him.

"Wait until you see the sequel."

When they entered Cedar Grove Cemetery, the two Trappists were far ahead, moving along at a brisk pace, and in the middle distance, Roger Knight's golf cart, he at the wheel, Professor Chadwick as copilot, was just making the turn at the sexton's building. Backhoes and other cemetery machinery stood half hidden in a fenced-off area to the right. From the open doors of the sexton's shed, several men stared out at them, the cemetery grounds crew. Beth looked at them as Roger had. One of them, wearing a Cubs cap, turned abruptly away, but not before Beth recognized him. So Q had come to the funeral after all.

They arrived at the gravesite. On the road beside it, the hearse and another black vehicle were parked. The casket already stood on a lowering device over the open grave. Father Carmody, wearing a cope now from which a gorgeous stole emerged, waited impatiently. Philip Knight stood with another man a few feet off. Then they all gathered around the grave.

The words Father Carmody read were whipped away by a breeze that had sprung up, the ribbon marker in his book fluttering like a pennant. Beth looked down into the scarcely concealed hole, and all the consoling ceremonies could not disguise the grim fact that they were going to put David Williams into the ground and cover his casket with dirt. She inhaled deeply and lifted her eyes to the old priest, who was having trouble preventing the breeze from turning the pages of his prayer book. Jay Williams had been directed to a place immediately to the right of Father Carmody. Beth noticed the man Mame had identified as Briggs on the edge of the little group, seemingly keeping a distance from Mame. What would she say if she saw him? How could she not? She had slipped off one shoe and stood somewhat lopsided next to Beth.

Roger Knight was distracted as he stood beside Chadwick. Looking across the grave at Jay Williams, he recalled Phil's speculation. Amanda stood just behind him, her eyes wide with unease. Jay had worried about his father, ostensibly because of the effects of the financial meltdown on him. He did not think that was the sole explanation of his father's behavior, though, and had actually asked if Phil could find out what was wrong. He had apparently turned to Ziggy Cobalt as an alternative. If so, Jay would have found out disturbing things. That his father had been interested in Mame Childers must have devastated his son, who thought it a betrayal of his mother. How deep had his resentment been?

One thing, however, had been cleared up. It was the presence of an unidentified Notre Dame student at Gethsemani that had provided the middle term for Phil's speculation about Jay Williams. That student had been a reporter for the *Irish Rover*, who had gone to the monastery in the hope of interviewing Brother Joachim. The events in the hermitage had made that impossible. The intrepid reporter had not known of those events—what a scoop he might have had—except indirectly. When his request was denied, he beat it back to South Bend to write a story about his failure to interview the Notre Dame grad who had become a Trappist monk.

Beside Roger, Chadwick was leaning over his walker. He should have stayed in the golf cart. "I want to check out the neighborhood, Roger. Our plot is near here."

The neighborhood now included two elegant mausolea, which blocked the view of the golden dome from where they stood. What must it be like to know the exact place where one would eventually be laid to rest?

Father Carmody had closed his book and was now vigorously sprinkling holy water on the casket. He then passed the sprinkler to Jay.

Roger felt a tap on his shoulder and turned. Phil. His brother moved his head, and Roger stepped back. Phil whispered that the distinguished stranger standing a few feet off, of the group but not in it, was Wilfrid Childers, keeping his distance. Had he recognized Phil from their encounter in Connecticut?

"Timothy Quinn seems to have joined the sexton's crew, Phil."

"He's here?"

Quinn had emerged from the sexton's shed and now stood ten yards away, even less in the group than the elegant Wilfrid Childers who had caught Phil's attention.

"Right over there."

Phil immediately left Roger's side and started toward him. His manner must have alerted Quinn. He started, turned, and then began to move rapidly back along the road, Phil in pursuit. Quinn started to run, a mistake. Phil quickly caught up with him and took him by the arm, saying something. Quinn wrenched his arm free and began to run again. Roger thought it was overly dramatic of Phil to bring the fellow down with a tackle. No doubt the influence of the *genius loci*. Off to the east was the great stadium that Rockne had built and Lou Holtz had enlarged. Jimmy Stewart had joined Phil and was now manacling their captive. Roger sighed.

Beth Hanrahan had witnessed all this and was deeply upset. She came to Roger and grabbed his sleeve. "What are they doing with Q?"

Roger looked into her eyes, at the graying still-lovely hair, at the woman who had given her life to the downtrodden. "I think they want to talk to him."

"About what?"

For answer, Roger let his eyes drift to the casket.

"That's ridiculous!"

"I'm going with Maurice," Emil Chadwick said, and Roger nodded. Beth was hurrying to where Quinn was in the custody of Jimmy Stewart.

"Where in the name of God is he going?" Mame asked in a tight voice. Her question seemed addressed to Roger. She was glaring at the man who had moved farther from the gravesite, strolling off on the road away from the sexton's shed.

"Who is he?"

"Wilfrid. My husband," Mame said. "Of course, all this ceremony is strange to him."

Behind the wheel of his golf cart, Roger moved quickly after Wilfrid. The man jumped when Roger came up beside him; of course, the vehicle made no sound.

"Mr. Childers. Hop in."

He looked at Roger, he looked at the golf cart, and his surprise gave way to amusement. "You're Professor Knight."

"I'm afraid I am."

"Well, why not?" Childers said, settling himself on the seat beside Roger. Roger eased up on the brake pedal, and they began to move. The road made a turn and ran along the fence separating the cemetery from what was left of the sixteenth fairway. Where it turned again there was an entrance through which the hearse had entered the cemetery with the body of David Williams, the gates still open.

"You were a friend of David's?"

"One of his clients."

"Ah. Like your wife."

Childers nodded.

"Did Ziggy Cobalt tell you about me?"

An attempt at a puzzled smile.

"How did you know who I was?"

"Is it a secret?" He managed to laugh.

"It is a very risky thing to hire a private detective, Mr. Childers. Particularly one like Ziggy Cobalt. They can become curious about your curiosity, and you become the watched rather than the watcher."

"Interesting."

"My brother has known Ziggy for years. I suppose you had him tracing David Williams? All the way to Kentucky?" Roger dropped his eyes. "Those aren't the best shoes for walking in the woods, are they? Of course, any shoe leaves its distinctive imprint. You have made some rather sizable blunders. Including registering at the guesthouse as Briggs."

Childers had been listening intently to what Roger said, amusement giving way to caution. Now he reached for and got control of the wheel of the cart, putting his foot over Roger's and depressing the pedal. They shot through the gate and onto the campus road. Childers removed the key and hopped out of the cart, studying Roger. Then he went rapidly around the cart, pushed Roger across the seat, and reinserted the key. "Let's go look at the lakes."

"Why did you come to the funeral?"

"To make sure the sonofabitch was dead."

Jimmy Stewart had put through a call on his cell phone, and a South Bend patrol car was on its way to take Timothy Quinn downtown for questioning.

"Questions?" Quinn asked. "What questions? Ask them here." Beth was at his side, hugging his arm.

"You shouldn't have gone to Gethsemani, Quinn."

The man's mouth fell open. The subsequent smile revealed discolored teeth. "Is that the charge, visiting a monastery?"

"That, and hitting your old classmate over the head with a piece of firewood."

You never know how a killer will react when he's caught. Quinn at least showed some originality.

"Let's go to the sexton's shed first. I should punch out."

The patrol car slid into the cemetery road, and Jimmy led Quinn away.

"I'll be down as soon as I can," Phil said and started back to the grave. Mame Childers came hobbling toward him.

"Where's my brother?" Phil asked her. "The fat man in a golf cart."

"He has given my husband a lift! And I can scarcely walk."

Then Phil saw Roger, with a passenger beside him, disappear through the gate. What the hell?

Phil loped away, a stitch in his side. The pursuit of Quinn had taught him how out of shape he was. When he reached the gate, he saw the golf cart going around a curve and then out of sight. At that moment, the hearse came through the gate, about to leave. Phil flagged it down. The driver was surprised to be asked for a lift, but Phil hopped in as he made his request. "Just go along this road, and step on it."

"Who are you?"

Phil rolled to the side, got out his wallet, opened it, and flashed it at the driver. "I'm a detective."

"Jesus," the driver exclaimed and stepped on it.

They made the turn and went past the practice putting green and then Rockne Memorial. There was a stop sign at Dorr Road, which led to the highway. Phil flipped a coin in his head and said, "Straight ahead."

The lake came into view, and then they were on the road that passed the Log Chapel.

"Stop!" Phil cried. He already had the door open. He piled out and went running toward the chapel.

Roger was at the wheel of the golf cart, with which he had pinned a man to the wall of the chapel. The man, struggling, cursing, could not free himself. Roger seemed to be inching forward, increasing the pressure as Phil came up.

"What's going on?"

"Meet the murderer of David Williams, Phil."

EPILOGUE

ROGER WADDLED INTO THE ROOM WHERE PHIL AND Jimmy Stewart were watching television, considered one of the beanbag chairs, thought better of it, and lowered himself onto the middle cushion of a couch.

"What's on?"

He was ignored. He was not offended. His own mind was still full of the commentary by Cornelius a Lapide he had just been reading, that on Psalm 87, a reminder of the fragility of life, the shortness of our days. He must tell Jay Williams what good company writing that initial message had put him in. *Your days are numbered.* That in effect had been Brother Joachim's salutary reminder to his classmate. That Joachim had been there at David Williams's bedside when he died was a comforting thought, almost a reconciliation scene.

Winter had come and gone; new life greenly put in its appearance on the campus; the game on the screen was baseball. The seasons of the athletic liturgical year succeeded one another, although with some overlapping, to the delight of Phil and Jimmy.

The jurisdictional dispute as to where Wilfrid Childers would be tried, and indeed for what, went on. Meanwhile, Jacuzzi, the local prosecutor, had brought a charge of kidnapping against the suave New Yorker for carrying Roger off as he had. Childers's lawyer had countered with a charge of assault and battery against Roger.

"Well, the cart is battery driven," Roger mused.

Childers's mistake was to have left the ignition key in place when he tried to pull Roger from the cart. He succeeded only in pulling him behind the wheel. Roger released the brake and for several minutes pursued Childers about the lawn below the Log Chapel. It was when Childers had attempted to leap onto the abbreviated hood of the cart that Roger was able to pin him helplessly against the wall of the chapel. Given the outcome, Jacuzzi was not sanguine about the kidnapping charge.

Jacuzzi had gone to Kentucky and passed pointless hours there. Emptor, the county prosecutor, was an auctioneer in his spare time, which seemed to be considerable, and did not give Jacuzzi comfort. "Sheriff Casper knows nothing about it."

Childers's lawyer had chuckled when Jacuzzi told him about the cast of the footprints found at the back door of the hermitage; wearing latex gloves, he handled the chunk of firewood as if he were about to go to bat. He shook his head. "Not heavy enough."

That might have described all the evidence, since it was all circumstantial. Had Wilfrid Childers signed in at the Gethsemani guesthouse as Larry Briggs? The guest master, shown photographs of the two men, pointed to Childers when asked which was Briggs, but Jacuzzi was not charmed by the thought of putting a monk on the stand.

"He'll get away with murder," Jacuzzi wailed. As a prosecutor he must have known how unfortunately common an outcome that was. The criminal justice system is an imperfect substitute for the Last Judgment.

Meanwhile, Mame had been reconciled with her husband. That she herself had been the occasion for his putative actions had its effect on her. Her former husband was thought to have killed her lover. It came to seem almost Shakespearean. "Allegedly killed," she would add primly.

"The woman has become a moral theologian," Father Carmody complained. "Apparently, she has wearied of canon law."

The intricacies of human action, the murkiness of responsibility, the sea of contingencies in which we live our days, of all these Mame Childers had become the poet.

"He was driven out of his mind," she explained to the priest. No need to say by what. Ah, the fatal susceptibility of the masculine heart. When she wasn't instructing Father Carmody in moral theology, she was advising her husband's lawyers. Yes, husband. The reconciliation had been total. Father Carmody had been approached on the matter, but in the end Mame and Wilfrid were united in holy matrimony by Monsignor Sparrow. Wilfrid, of course, was out on bail.

"Peace to them," Carmody muttered. *"Pox eis*, that is." And he spelled it for Roger.

The Old Bastards in Leahy's Lounge gave all these matters their full attention. They had not been impressed by the funeral of David Williams.

"White vestments!" Horvath cried. "There wasn't a moist eye in the church."

Armitage Shanks began to chant the *Dies Irae* but found that he had forgotten the words.

"You see? We'll be forgetting the Our Father soon."

The sequel to the burial buoyed them up. The fat Professor

Knight being carried off by the killer and then pinning his abductor to the wall of the Log Chapel—that was a scene to which they could relate.

"We must all get such carts," Potts said. "We can roam the campus looking for administrators."

The prospect of pinning vice presidents and provosts and deans to campus walls and trees excited them.

"Do you need a license to drive one of them?" Bingham asked.

"You already have a driver's license, Horvath."

"It's restricted."

"Hang him high," Potts growled. Doubtless he was remembering the campus petition to show clemency to Wilfrid Childers.

"He'll get off scot-free."

"What is the meaning of that word, scot-free?"

Armitage Shanks launched into an explanation, but Murph arrived at last with their drinks.

"Feeding time," he said cheerfully.

Events had of course led to the abandonment of plans to stage a revival of *Behind the Bricks*, and Hazel was furious. Jay and Amanda went to explain.

"After all the trouble I took." She glared at Amanda, but her expression softened when she turned to Jay.

"It's all your fault, Hazel."

"My fault?"

"You turned down the part I offered you."

The cancellation complemented the cancellation of Casey Winthrop's lecture. The *Irish Rover* had begun a three-part series on the life and work of Casey Winthrop '89, but it was not the same thing.

Jay and Amanda planned to visit the author when they went to Florida on spring break.

"The sequel to *Tumbleweed* has appeared," Jay said.

"What's it called?"

"*Cactus.*"

"Any good?"

"How can you ask?"

Fenway in the Notre Dame Foundation had approached Jay about his father's offer to fund a new ethics center. Jay told them he had other plans.

"Some other building?"

"Yes."

Fenway sat eagerly forward.

"In Minneapolis," Jay said.

On an early April morning Beth Hanrahan was hurrying back from Mass at Holy Rosary. Father Romanus had told her he was offering it for the repose of David Williams's soul. Another? Beth was surprised, but Romanus explained this was not the Mass she had requested long ago. "Buy one, get one free."

"I didn't give a stipend."

"Don't be so literal."

Returning from Notre Dame to Our Lady of the Road had been in many ways a relief. Q drove her back, muttering about the indignity of his arrest by Jimmy Stewart. As for Phil Knight, Q complained that it hadn't been a clean tackle.

"Will you stay?" She meant in Minneapolis.

Thought went on beneath the Cubs cap. "Either that or reenlist in the army."

"I'll take that for yes."

Once it had seemed that the only one of them who was leading a more or less normal life was David Williams. Now Beth would cast Casey Winthrop for that role. What a lovely woman Peaches was. And the baby!

The baby. Father Carmody baptized Casey and Peaches's baby in the Log Chapel before they fled again to the warmth of Florida. Then it was time for Beth's request. The old priest had been agreeable to her suggestion that they include Brother Joachim in the little ceremony by the Log Chapel. So, two days after David's funeral, at the crack of dawn, the three of them had stood over the spot where so many years ago she and Joachim had buried her miscarried child. Joachim recited the *De profundis*, while Beth tried unsuccessfully to hold back the tears. Father Carmody sprinkled the boulder that Joachim had replaced, and all withdrew.